# lasso lovebirds

A Rainbow Ranch Novella

## clio evans

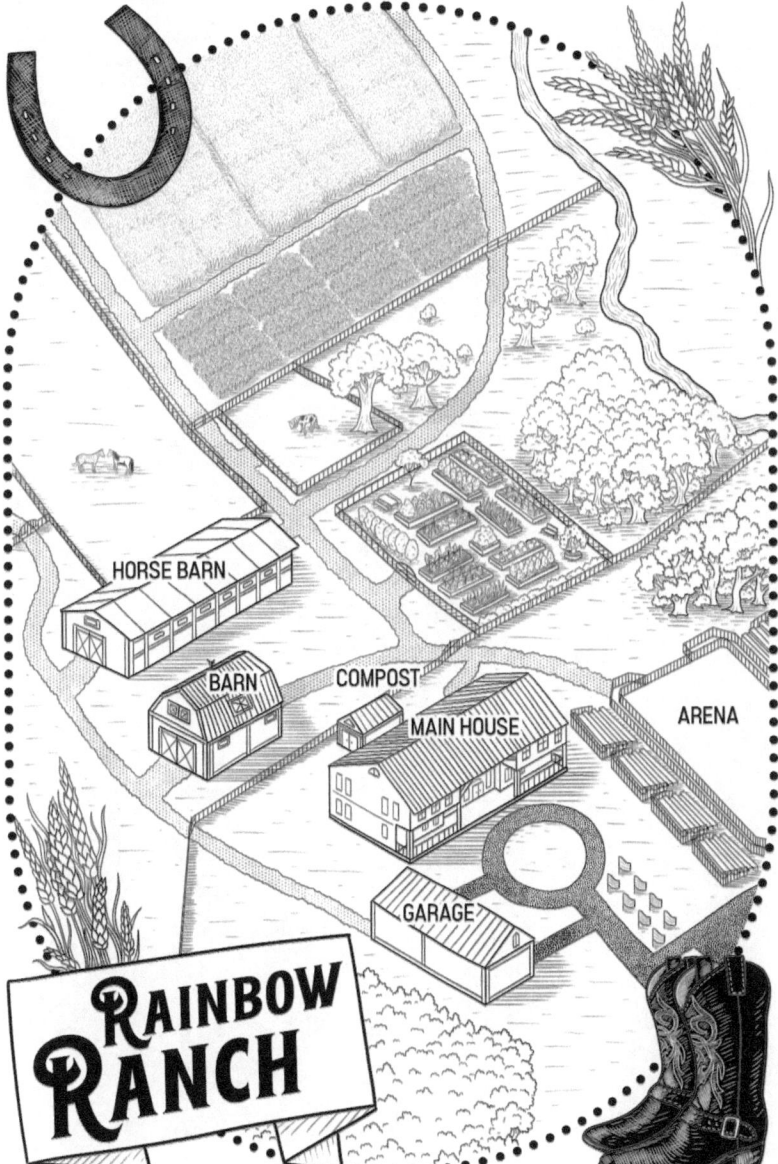

HORSE BARN

BARN

COMPOST

MAIN HOUSE

ARENA

GARAGE

RAINBOW RANCH

# content warnings

Howdy, Partner. *Lasso Lovebirds* contains the following:

- Parental death from car wreck (happened in past, discussed, accident not on page)
- Discussions of mental health and grief
- Discussions of homophobia
- *Detailed* sex scenes with: BDSM Dom/sub dynamics, praise kink, spanking, Shibari, Sybian Saddle, oral sex, threesomes, squirting, throat fucking, sex toys, and more.

If you have any questions regarding content warnings, please reach out to me clioevansauthor@gmail.com

# 1
# beau

IN MY EXPERIENCE, things always happened in threes. As my boot squelched into the third pile of horse shit this morning, I had to wonder if the universe was just pokin' fun at me. A curse wrenched from my lips, and I glanced around out of habit for any of the teens on our ranch—even though I was most assuredly alone.

If one of them caught wind of me cursing, I'd never hear the end of it. The good news was that the sun had barely risen, and while I wasn't the only one up this early, I *was* the only one trudging through a field to fix the fence's wiring before the rain hit.

"Damn it," I muttered, kicking my heel out.

Shit plopped into the wet mud, the ground damp from the constant storms we'd had over the last couple weeks. Thunder rumbled in the distance as I crossed from the stables to my truck. I got in, shutting the door quietly and cranking the engine.

I hoped I could knock this out quickly to make it back in time for breakfast. Otherwise there'd be hell to pay from my twin brother, Boone.

Of the four of us, Boone was the only sibling that could wrangle me indoors. Maybe it was the sticky buns or maybe it was the fact that we'd shared the same womb, but he always managed to *know* when something was off with me. Just how I knew the same about him. It was a sixth sense. Which was why I needed to fix my attitude—and clean off my boots real good—before walking through the dining room door.

As the eldest, the weight of running the ranch and always having the right answers sat on my broad, sun-tanned shoulders. I rarely got a moment alone, which was why I often jumped on tasks like this. Mending a fence before dawn meant I could have a little time to myself to ponder, dream, and spiral.

What was putting my hackles up this morning wasn't the fact that I'd just stepped in a pile of shit. And it wasn't because of the storm brewing just a few miles north, or even the usual pressure of being the boss.

It was something else entirely.

I turned on the radio as I rumbled down the dirt road, using the few minutes of peace to think.

Ever since Boone and Wylie had fallen for each other, I'd been reminded of the fact that I was painfully alone. And it was silly, right? I was so damn happy for the two of them that it hurt. Hell, we all were. They were perfect for each other. Billie, our younger sister, and Benny—the youngest of the four of us—thought so too.

Romance was in the air. And while it was beautiful and heart-warming, it reminded me of the secrets I'd been keeping. It reminded me of the deep pining I had for someone I *couldn't* have, and how I'd probably end up growing old alone.

Rainbow Ranch was the love of my life, right? That had to be enough to fill the cavernous ache echoing in my chest.

My headlights beamed through the grape-crushed dawn as I slowed to a stop. The marker I'd placed the other day to show where the fencing needed repair shot up in the grass. I turned off the truck and hopped out.

I tightened my tool belt as I trudged over to the fence. This patch-up was right near the front gate, which was exactly why I'd wanted it done so fast. I couldn't have our fences lookin' rundown, especially when it was visible from the paved road.

Three flags billowed as the wind whipped up—a brilliant rainbow, a bright pink, blue, and white, and our symbol: a horseshoe with two R's and a rainbow connecting them, representing Rainbow Ranch. I scowled, slamming my hand down on top of my cowboy hat before it was blown straight off by the breeze.

"Damn," I muttered, my brows shooting up.

I came prepared with my fence stretcher, fencing sleeves, pliers, and a set of gloves. But as I started to tug on the gloves, the wind slammed into me again, this time whisking my hat straight off my head and tumbling into the field.

"Damn it!" I yelled, stumbling forth to catch it before it went to our neighbor's property.

Booming thunder made the hair stand up on the back of my neck. Headlights blinked on the paved road, drawing my attention. A raindrop plopped against my forehead right as a white van with saucers on top—*are those satellites?*—pulled up.

The van kicked up gravel as it skidded to a halt in front of the gate. The last of the sunrise was clipped by dark, roiling clouds. My eyes widened as I realized a wall was

3

forming in the sky. *Surely that's not what I think it is.* The wind was growing violent, causing the flags to thrash.

Someone with bright green hair hopped out of the vehicle, waving their hands wildly. They pointed to the sky, and my stomach dropped as the clouds began to swirl in a way I knew all too well.

Living in Oklahoma, tornadoes weren't all that rare. But one forming right here on the ranch? I couldn't remember the last time that'd happened.

"Do you need help?" I shouted, already rushing toward the gate.

"Can I drive in?" they yelled back. "It's coming in fast!"

My chest constricted and I nodded, unlatching the chain quickly. The metal groaned as I fought to swing it open, my heart thumpin' so loud I could hear it over the storm.

The stranger hopped back into their van and floored the gas, launching over the cattle gate and onto our graveled road.

They rolled down the window. "Get in," they shouted.

*Gosh, they're pretty to look at.* I swallowed hard and pointed at my truck. "Follow me to the ranch."

When I looked back up at the sky, my stomach twisted just like the funnel forming. We needed to get to the house. *Now.*

I sprinted to my truck and launched into the front seat, slamming the door shut. The tires peeled over the gravel as large raindrops pelted the windshield, the wind rocking the cabin as I whipped around to speed back toward the ranch.

My gaze flicked to the rearview. The stranger was speeding right behind me, as if the devil were breathing down our necks.

"*Fuck.*" The funnel touched the ground behind us.

It was gonna land. Now the question was whether or not it'd follow us.

It'd been a long time since we'd had a storm season quite like this, and the thought of Rainbow Ranch being swept away by a tornado was a worry I had every year. Everything could be gone in the blink of an eye, and then what? What would I do? What would *we* do?

I wasn't religious. Never had been, never would be. But still, I sent up a silent prayer, a wish, a hope. All I wanted was for them to be safe. My family. The ranch. The animals.

The truck jerked. My knuckles whitened as I gripped the steering wheel, my boot pushing the pedal into the floorboard.

Even going this fast, it'd take a few more minutes to get back to the house. Adrenaline was a wild bronco in my veins, the earth torn up piece by piece by the tornado behind us. Sweat dripped down my back, my body trembling as we raced against mother nature.

"Please go. Please let up. *Please*."

My throat was dry. Every muscle in my body was so rigid, I knew I'd hurt tomorrow.

The horse stables loomed in the distance. My eyes darted from what was in front of me to the horror behind me.

Fuck. *Fuck*, we were gonna be okay.

The funnel was going a different way. I slowed down, trembling as I pulled to a stop on the road. I blew out a slow, deliberate breath as the stranger stopped behind me.

"*Fuck. Shit. Damn it*. What the fuck?!" I needed to get all the curses out while I could.

I kicked open the door and stepped onto the road, my

knees feeling like Boone's strawberry jelly. The stranger got out, raking their fingers through their green hair.

I approached them, a lump forming in my throat. Maybe it was just the storm that had me all riled up, but there was just something about them that was undeniably *hot*.

"Well, that was one hell of a way to meet someone," they said, offering a smile.

I couldn't help but grin. "I'm Beau Adams."

They held out a hand. "Sky Williams." They turned their head to look at the retreating clouds, their expression turning wistful. "Wish I could have grabbed a few pictures of that one. Glad it went the other way though, otherwise we would have been sitting ducks. I take it this is Rainbow Ranch?"

The corner of my mouth tugged as I shook their hand. Their skin was mighty soft against my calluses. "What gave it away?"

Sky planted their hands on their hips. "Well, for starters, you're the only ranch I've seen in hours with the pride flag and trans flag at the gate. Plus, I've *heard* of this place."

I raised a brow. "Good things? Bad things?" A lot of locals had a lot to say about us, and depending on who you got the story from, it was either about Rainbow Ranch being a paradise or *liberal hell*. "Are you looking for a place to stay?"

"Well," they hesitated. "Maybe? Johnson Springs didn't exactly feel like the friendliest place for a nonbinary person. Not that anywhere in this state really is..."

"You'll be safe here," I promised.

Sky cleared their throat, their pretty brown eyes dropping down. I realized I was still holding their hand. Their cheeks flushed as I released them, taking a step back.

"Sorry," I added. "I think I'm a little scatterbrained from the storm." What the hell was this heat creeping up the back of my neck?

"That was a close call," they agreed.

"How about you come in for breakfast with everyone and we can talk afterward? Could use some food after that scare. My brother makes the best breakfast in the state."

Sky's dimples pressed into their apple cheeks. "Now, that's a bold claim, cowboy."

"Well," I chuckled. "I'll let you be the judge of that. Welcome to Rainbow Ranch, Sky."

# 2
# sky

BEAU WAS nothing like I'd expected.

When I'd heard about Rainbow Ranch from one of the locals in the town nearby, they talked about Beau like he was an old, tough cowboy. And while he was probably tough and definitely a cowboy, he was also a gorgeous, sun-kissed man with kind hazel eyes and a jawline I envied.

I felt out of place as I got out of my van and waited for him to grab his things. The farmhouse before us was massive, with a wraparound front porch and weathered paint peeling from the slats. My head craned back as I looked to the sky, my fingers itching to grab my camera. Some of the most magical lighting in the world happened after a storm, as if it were some sort of offering of hope after devastating destruction.

It was stupid to go storm chasing alone. But, after falling out with my assistant last week, I'd taken to the Oklahoma countryside alone in search of storm cells to photograph. When the radar had promised something good around four a.m., I'd loaded up my single suitcase and hit the road for the ranch, hoping to catch a funnel.

All I'd caught was trouble. Plain and simple. Thankfully, I'd made it to the ranch, and Beau was there to let me in.

"You alright there, Sky?" His sweet timbre drawl made my heart skip a beat.

"Yeah. Just thinking."

Beau offered a smile and gestured to the house. "Let's get inside. We're late and I'm never gonna hear the end of it."

I followed him up the front steps to the door. It squeaked on its hinges as he opened it, stepping inside.

"Well, well, well. Look who decided to join us."

A man who looked *exactly* like Beau materialized in front of us wearing an apron and wielding a wooden spoon. Beau held up his hands.

"There was a storm. Or did you miss that while you were cooking? Also, we have a guest. Boone, this is Sky." He turned, giving me space to shake the other man's hand. "Sky, this is Boone, my twin brother."

"Oh." *Twins.* That made sense.

Boone's attitude warmed immediately. "Hi there, welcome. We got plenty of food on the table. Would you like a cup of coffee? Orange juice? I got some fancy sparkling water in, too—"

"I can get it for myself," I said quickly. "You don't need to make me anything. I'm intruding—"

"Nonsense." He waved the spoon like it was a wand and he was a Southern fairy. "I'm the cook here. It's what I do. And you're not intruding at all. I'm just here to give my older brother a hard time."

The door opened quickly behind me and I squeaked as Beau acted fast, yanking me out of the way before it could bump my behind. I turned right as a gorgeous woman stepped inside with a scowl, her denim shirt damp.

I was no better than a man. The way it clung to her body short-circuited my brain. A few natural curls stuck to her face, the rest pulled back into a claw clip. She had warm brown skin and was taller than me by at least a few inches.

Was everyone on Rainbow Ranch this beautiful? Between Beau and her, my little enby bisexual heart was losing it. My pulse thumped wildly, all words failing me.

"Well, well, well," Boone drawled. "Look who *also* decided to show up."

"Oh, don't even start," she hissed. "Did you see that damn tornado? I thought we were going to lose the whole ranch for a second there."

"Everyone else made it to breakfast on time, even with the storm," Boone said sweetly.

She glowered at him. "You know I'm going to lose my mind if I lose my crops this year. And you best be nice, Boone Adams, since your job as a cook depends on mine as a gardener. Where else are you going to get all the goods?"

Beau let out a hearty laugh, his gaze warm with familiarity. It was clear he'd heard this sort of banter a thousand times before. "Okay, okay. Break it up. Priscilla, this is Sky. Our guest. We just survived that tornado. I'm glad you're okay, too."

Her brown eyes flickered to us, her expression melting some. "Hi," she said, holding out her hand. "I'm Priscilla. You can call me Pris. What a hell of a morning to come to Rainbow Ranch, huh?"

"Yeah," I squeaked.

"Are you a cowboy?" she asked. "Cowgirl? Cow*they*?"

That made me snort. "None of the above, though I suppose cowthey would be the one. I'm a storm chaser."

Pris cocked her head. "Interesting. I thought storm chasers were just a thing in the movies."

I laughed. "I promise we're real. I photograph the cells. There's still a lot to learn about why tornadoes happen, and getting photographic evidence can make a huge difference." My love of storms went all the way back to my childhood. Out of the rubble of a small dusty town, I'd taken my past and turned it into something good.

"Isn't that dangerous to be doing alone?" Beau asked quietly.

My cheeks warmed. I became painfully aware of the fact that I was standing between the two of them.

Boone cleared his throat and gave his brother a look I couldn't read. "I'm gonna go get started on that cup of coffee." He spun around and started whistling a tune, earning an eye roll from Beau.

Pris shook her head. "They do that a lot. The twin telepathic link. Then there's Billie and Benny, and when the four of them get going, it's something else."

"*Four?*" I echoed.

She smiled. "How about you come sit next to me, storm chaser?"

I glanced up at Beau and he nodded. "Let's go get some food, and we can talk some more about your stay."

A weight lifted off my shoulders. Already, this place felt better than Johnson Springs. Traveling alone the last couple weeks had left me feeling especially vulnerable. Even with the close call this morning, I felt ten times safer.

Rainbow Ranch was already living up to its reputation.

Beau and Pris led me through the doorway to the dining room. All eyes swiveled to the three of us. I hadn't realized just how many people were here.

"This is Sky," Pris said, gently taking my elbow and

guiding me to an empty chair. I appreciated her taking the lead, especially since I was a stranger showing up on their doorstep. "Here, we'll get seated. Boone will bring some coffee."

"Hi Sky," a woman at the end of the table said. She was clearly Boone and Beau's sister, even if she didn't have the identical features those two did. Although their vibes were different enough I could tell them apart with ease. "I'm Billie. This is Benny."

The man sitting next to her offered a kind smile. "Howdy."

"Hi," I said.

"I'm Winnie," a woman said as she entered the dining room with three mugs of coffee. She sat one down in front of me and Pris, then shoved the other one into Beau's hands.

He sighed happily. "Thanks, Winnie. Also, this is Wylie, Boone's partner."

I nodded toward the tough looking man currently biting into one of the biggest cinnamon rolls I'd ever seen. He waved his hand. "Welcome," he said.

"And then last but not least, this is Pepper, Eren, Tyler, and Jake," Beau said.

Four teens sat around the massive table with food piled onto their plates. From what I knew about Rainbow Ranch, which was only what I'd briefly read online while in Johnson Springs, it was a dude ranch, but it was also a place for foster kids to connect in a safe place. The entire operation made me feel emotional for several reasons, which was why it'd been a no-brainer to at least stop for a visit.

"Beau, do we have to work today if there's rain?" Pepper asked.

"Yep," he said. "Ranch life never stops. Maybe we'll do some fence repairs once the storm passes."

As if in response, a low rumble echoed through the house, rattling the windows.

"We should go check on the horses," Wylie said, glancing at Benny.

"You mean, make sure Dennis hasn't escaped?" Billie asked.

"Yes," everyone said in agreement.

"Dennis is a menace," Pris said next to me, grinning. "He's a mini horse with a personality the size of Texas."

"Oh," I said, pulling my coffee mug close.

The heat radiated through the ceramic, grounding me, as everyone started to chat amongst themselves. Wylie and Benny headed out the door despite the weather.

Just like that, I felt . . .

Normal.

No one asked why my hair was green. No one stared at me too long or made rude comments or made wild assumptions about who I was. They didn't treat me any differently or like I was a little freak.

They just existed.

And I existed alongside them.

My throat burned. Pris glanced over at me and her eyes softened. "Rainbow Ranch is good," she said. "I felt the same way the first time I came here."

I drew in a deep breath and nodded. "I don't know what came over me. Probably the adrenaline wearing off."

"Well, let's get some food in you. Sweet or savory or both?"

"Both," I said, blushing as she grabbed my plate and started to pile food on it. Beau had yet to sit down, his brows furrowed as he chatted in a low tone with one of the teens.

They weren't afraid of him. I wondered what that was like—being a teen who wasn't afraid of the very masculine man in the room?

My eyes had a mind of their own, roaming down to his denim-clad ass.

Beau's ass looked damn good in well-worn Wranglers.

*What is wrong with me?!*

Pris put my plate down with a wink and then filled hers with food. My mouth watered as I inhaled the homey, comforting scents, a blend that made my stomach growl.

*Oh my god.* A giant cinnamon roll sat on the edge of my plate. Or maybe it was some other type of bun? The icing on top looked a little different than what I was used to.

Boone swooped back through the dining room, his eyes lighting up when he saw my plate.

"Those are my famous buns," he said with a broad grin.

One of the teens giggled. "Boone's buns."

He clacked a set of tongs he had in his hands. "My famous cinnamon orange buns. Let me know how you like them."

"They're the best," Billie chimed.

I picked up the bun, the bread soft and squishy between my fingers, icing dripping to the plate. I sank my teeth in and moaned as the flavors burst across my tongue.

Boone's buns were heavenly.

"Good, right?" Pris asked. "I'll be riding the sugar high all day."

I would be too.

Between listening to everyone chat about this morning's storm and eating the delicious food—breakfast flew by. Once I polished my plate, I stood to gather dishes, Pris shook her head.

"I got this, we'll clean up. Seems like you have some business with Beau." She raised a brow at him.

I glanced up at the cowboy, meeting his warm gaze and feeling a heated tug in my stomach. Just the feeling of his eyes on me burned like a shot of whiskey. What was it about him? About the *two* of them? What if they were a couple?

Beau pushed back his chair and rose, taking his cup of coffee with him. "Looks like the rain cleared. Let's take a walk and talk?"

I nodded. "Okay, but are you sure I can't help—"

"We've got it, storm chaser," Pris chided.

"We do," Billie agreed, stacking dishes on top of each other. The teens were doing the same.

Beau smiled and tilted his head toward the front door. "Come on, Sky."

God, I was going to melt into the floor if he kept saying my name like that. A blush crept over my cheeks. I stole one last glance at the table, watching how easily everyone worked together, like a well oiled machine, then followed Beau out the door, his boots thumping on the creaky hardwood floor.

The air outside was still. Peaceful. My gaze swept to the distance where lightning danced in dark, swollen clouds— all heading *away* from us.

With it being storm season, there'd be plenty more like it.

Beau leaned against the porch railing and raised a brow. "So. What can we do for you, Sky?"

*Here goes nothing.* "Well, I'd like a place to stay for the next three weeks. Just to make it through storm season, then I'll be out of your hair. I'm happy to pay for lodging."

"If you're willing to work around the ranch instead, you don't need to pay."

*What?* That would be ideal. Saving money was never a bad idea. Growing up the way I did taught me to hold onto every penny earned . . . unless I was splurging on a new camera.

The thing was, I'd never worked a ranch. I was a hard worker, but had no idea what I could contribute to make it worth Beau's time. "I love that idea, but I've never worked on a ranch before. And I'd need to be able to leave at a moment's notice if there's a storm nearby."

"Have you ever done any gardening? Cooking? Anything like that?"

"Some gardening. I also take direction very well." *That* came out way different than I'd meant it to. Now, I was definitely blushing.

His cheeks were pink too. "I'm sure you do."

Tension rumbled between us. He rubbed the back of his neck, his breath hitching.

"If you want, you could help Pris out when you have the time. Pris is part of the reason this ranch even makes money. She's incredibly smart and runs everything to do with agriculture here. All of that food Beau makes? Rainbow Ranch is very farm-to-table, and we can thank her for that. She could use the help. I know we're in storm season and that's what you're here for, but you could still go chasing whenever you need to. Is that safe to do alone?"

"Not exactly." I winced. "I had a falling-out with my assistant and he left." It was the bare-bones version of what happened, but I'd leave it at that.

"Oh, I see," he said. "Well . . . I'd offer to help, but I'm usually needed around here."

The thought of storm chasing with a handsome cowboy like Beau made my heart go pitter-patter.

"Maybe I can take you out at some point," I said. "If you ever have a spare moment."

Another easy, sweet smile. "Well, if I got a spare moment, it'll be yours, Sky."

A throat cleared, startling both of us. I spun to see Pris standing there, her expression unreadable.

Beau swallowed hard and straightened, his tone hardening. "Sky is gonna be staying for a few weeks, and will help you out when they're not storm chasing. Can you show them to their room and around the ranch? I need to go . . . do things."

Pris crossed her arms, but nodded. "You got it, boss."

# 3
# priscilla

*Boss.*

Beau *was* the boss. That was a well-known fact. And yet, every time I called him boss, all I could think about was what it would be like to see Mr. Bossy Pants on his knees. Begging.

I'd never *ever* tell him about that little dream in a thousand years, though. Or that I'd been pining for the masked cowboy for years.

The first time I came to Rainbow Ranch, I was a teenager. Just like many of the foster kids that helped out, I'd come here to escape, only to find that the slower pace of life and long days of hard work were exactly what I needed. Then I'd left Oklahoma for a few years after graduation. I got a degree in Agronomy Management, met someone I thought I was going to love for the rest of my life, had my heart shattered, and came right back to the ranch.

Rainbow Ranch was home.

Coming back here, the little crush I'd had as a teen blossomed into something entirely different as an adult. The seven-year age gap between Beau and me no longer felt like too much—especially now that I was twenty-eight and he was thirty-five.

But Beau was *off limits*.

Still, I couldn't help but watch him walk away. I swallowed hard, trying to refocus on our guest—the attractive storm chaser with pretty eyes and bright green hair. They were a little bit shorter than me, a little bit curvier, and wore a look on their face that I knew all too well.

I'd never forget the first time I came to Rainbow Ranch, or the feeling of being accepted for who I was.

There was something special about this place, which was why I'd stayed here for so long and probably would stay here the rest of my life.

I loved the ranch, loved the people, loved our mission, and loved what we did here. I could make a lot more money elsewhere with my degree, but I was able to help people at Rainbow Ranch. And that made up for everything else.

Now, if only I could find someone to love.

"Let me help you grab your things," I said to Sky.

They shook their head. "You've already done enough. Let me grab my bag, it's just a suitcase. And then I'm all yours to help with whatever you need."

*All yours.* I hid my smirk as they went down the stairs to their van, yanking the door open to retrieve their things. I leaned against the post, watching them with interest.

There was something about them I just couldn't look away from. Maybe it was because they were a new face, or maybe it was because I saw the way Beau looked at them, or maybe it was because I saw the way they looked at *me*.

Regardless, I was interested.

I blamed Boone and Wylie. With their newfound love, it was hard not to think about what life could look like with someone by your side—that type of companionship I'd always craved. Those two were cavity-sweet together.

The thing was, I was polyamorous—which meant that not everyone would be open to the kind of connection I was looking for. On top of that, I really liked *solo* polyamory. I wanted to be able to make my bed the way I liked it, have my space the way I liked it, and do everything the way I liked it, but I still wanted to have meaningful relationships. I still wanted to fall in love and be loved.

I just would never be the domestic type, with one partner and a house full of kids, or any of the other things most people wanted.

I wanted to be loved, but I also still wanted to be *with* myself.

I would never put myself in a position again where I wasn't the one in control. I'd never be with someone who told me what to do, or didn't respect my decisions. I've already been there once, and the trauma from that son of a bitch had taken a lot of therapy and years to work past.

And there were still days where I wasn't over it. Those types of relationships ruined everything. That experience made me see each situation in a new light, and question everyone's motives around me. How much pain had I gone through, simply for loving the wrong person? Nathan had not been the Prince Charming I'd believed he was, but at least he was out of my life for good.

Rainbow Ranch healed those parts of me as well as it could, but opening myself up to someone new was frightening.

So instead, I spent my time pining for someone that would never love me back. And I hoped for the day where I would find the one—or *ones*—who would understand and accept the lifestyle I chose to live.

Was that so wrong?

To top *all* of that off, I was kinky. Not just a playful hair tug or a light slap on the ass type of kinky—but *actually* kinky. There were things that I liked to do in the bedroom . . . and living in a house full of other people didn't exactly offer the privacy I needed for any of them. I *loved* being a Domme. It turned me on to tie someone up and make them come over and over again until they were nothing but a little mess. It turned me on to spank them, push them, use them, and pleasure them.

And just to add another layer to the *Priscilla-never-finding-love* cake—my standards were high.

That was probably the real reason I would never find someone.

And why I was perfectly content only thinking of the new storm chaser as eye candy. A fling wasn't what I wanted, and it never would be.

So I would just admire them and dream about what could be, then move on with my life. They'd be in and out, just like the countless other people that had come through this ranch. We'd be nothing but a memory covered in a layer of Oklahoma dust and rainbow glitter.

Sky came back up the steps with their suitcase and glanced back at the van. "Should I be parking somewhere else?"

"I think it's fine there for now," I said. "Beau usually parks the truck closer to the barn, so I'm sure he'll have you move it. Let's go find you a room."

Before Sky could protest, I picked up their suitcase and found that it was way lighter than I'd expected. I carried it into the house with them right behind me, leading the way until we reached the long hallway.

"Beau's bedroom has a lasso on it," I said, gesturing toward the end of the hall.

"Oh," Sky said, cheeks flushing. "I guess that's good to know."

I smiled wistfully and slowed, rapping on the door to my bedroom. "This one is mine." I pointed at the door across from us. "And that can be yours. It's not too much. The rooms are humble, but they're cozy. And you get used to them."

Sky stepped past the threshold, head tilting as they looked around. I leaned in through the doorway and set their bag down, and then propped my shoulder against the frame.

"What do ya think?" I asked.

They smiled. "It'll do. Not too glamorous, but neither was the motel in Johnson Springs. And this is a lot safer."

My chest squeezed. "It is. If you ever need anything, I'm here. Although, I don't think you'll have any trouble out here."

They breathed out, their shoulders sinking.

"How about you take some time to get settled in? I'll give you some peace."

"I think I'd rather help you," Sky said. "I can settle in tonight, but I kind of interrupted your entire morning. And Beau told me you have lots of work to do."

"You just went through a tornado, and you want to work?" I raised a brow.

Sky shifted from side to side, then shrugged their shoulders. "If you don't mind."

"I don't. I just don't want you to feel like you have to. But, I suppose I can show you around the ranch. I already did most of my work before anyone was up, and I'll do more after lunch."

"Okay." Sky smiled and dragged their suitcase to the other side of the room, then pulled their phone out of their denim pocket. They made a face.

"Oh yeah," I said. "Cell service out here is rough. Beau has better internet access in his office if you need it."

"I will later," Sky said with a nod. "But it's fine for now. How on earth do y'all live out here without good cell service?"

"It's kind of nice sometimes," I said. "And frankly, I just sneak into Beau's office when I need to connect with the rest of the world. I have an Instagram account I started a couple years ago to post pictures from around the ranch."

They grinned. "Really? I'm sure people love it."

"For the most part," I chuckled. "Alright, Sky. Come with me."

"Yes, ma'am."

# 4

# beau

THE NEXT MORNING thankfully didn't start with a tornado.

I kissed Dolly's soft nose as I offered her an apple. It crunched as she bit into it, her tail swishing with the contented happiness I took pride in seeing from our horses. I rubbed my hand up the bridge of her nose, her hair soft as velvet. Dolly was my horse, a gorgeous Palomino Appaloosa mare with the temperament of sunshine and rainbows. She made a damn good roping partner, too.

"You're a good girl," I said softly. "Should I get you another? Probably shouldn't, huh? Everyone else will be jealous."

"Someone's lucky."

My head twisted in surprise. Sky stood in the doorway to the stables, their expression brightening as they looked around. I smiled as they came closer, their eyes darting to Dolly.

"Morning," I greeted. "How'd you sleep?"

"Good," they said. "Really good."

"Want to give her an apple?" I asked, pulling one from my pocket.

I'd never tire of seeing someone light up at the opportunity to interact with the horses. Sky grinned and took the apple, their fingertips brushing mine. Sparks skated across my skin, my breath hitching as they offered it to Dolly.

"Oh my god," they giggled as she bit into it. "Wow. She's so gentle."

"Have you ever been around horses? Or on a ranch?" I asked curiously.

"Nope. This would be the first." Their cheeks were rosy, and their wide smile made my chest flutter with butterflies. "I always wanted a horse growing up, though. Definitely told my parents at some point I'd grow up to be a cowgirl."

I chuckled. "You'd look good in my hat."

*Did I really just say that?* My pulse raced as Sky's sunny smile turned into a smirk.

"Are you flirtin' with me, Beau?" they asked.

My cheeks turned beet red. "I'm not very good at it, am I?"

"I think you're adequate," they teased. Their eyes skated from my hat down to my boots, heat tugging in my veins. "You're busy, I'm sure, but I'm still learning my way around here. Do you mind pointing me in the direction of the barn?"

Hell, I *was* busy. But . . .

"How about I give you another tour? If you'd like. Part of my job, really."

"Are you sure? I don't want to distract you. Pris did a great job showing me around yesterday, I'm just still getting my footing."

"You're a welcome distraction, Sky."

Good god, who was I, flirtin' like this? I swallowed hard as I rolled my shoulders back, my cheeks hotter than a fresh sunburn. Sky wiped their hands on their denim-clad thighs and then planted them on their hips, glancing around the barn.

"So this is the horse barn," I said. "We currently have ten horses, and then there's Dennis."

"Oh, I need to meet Dennis. Everyone talks about him. I feel like he has to be the size of Texas, but I haven't seen a horse that big . . ."

I barked out a laugh. "Oh no. Dennis barely reaches my knees. Come on. We'll go out to the pasture."

I led them through the double barn doors. Sunshine dappled our shoulders, warming us as we came to the fence. I rested my arms on the top and stole a glimpse at Sky as they climbed up onto the first rung. They leaned over, grinning as they took in the beauty of the pasture.

Everything was verdant green, the sky bright blue above us without a cloud in sight. You'd never know that we'd nearly been swept away yesterday.

A few of the horses roamed freely, nibbling at the grass.

And then there was Dennis.

The moment he spotted us, he came trotting over. Sky's laugh made my heart squeeze with joy. I climbed up the fence and dropped to the other side, holding out my hand for them.

They wobbled at the top and before they could tumble over, I gripped their hips and lifted them with ease. Sky's hands planted against my chest, their eyes wide as I put them down.

*Ba-dump, ba-dump.* My heart was beating out of my chest. Their lips looked so damn soft—I nearly leaned down to kiss them.

*Get a hold of yourself.*

Dennis ruined the moment by butting into my shin.

"Hey," I grunted and stepped back, shaking my head as I looked down at our famed miniature horse.

Dennis the menace, our pride and joy, and resident troublemaker.

"Welp," I said. "This is Dennis."

"Oh my god," Sky squeaked, bending over to pet the top of his head. "He's so cute. The cutest thing I've ever seen."

Dennis butted me again, snorting as they ruffled his dark mane. His glossy black coat glistened, clearly having been brushed today. I glanced up, spotting Benny across the way in the smaller pasture that was for riding horses. He was currently giving Sassafras, a beautiful brown mare, a good ride around.

"He does well at the rodeo," I chuckled.

"I'm sure. You know, I've never gone to a rodeo."

"Really? Well, you'll get to in a couple weeks if you're still here. There's also Y'all Pride Picnic the first weekend of June. Fingers crossed we get no storms. They're always a lot of fun."

"I'd like that," they said softly.

Dennis turned his full attention to them and my brows shot up as he gave a soft snort and softly nudged them. For such a tough little horse, he was being gentle.

Horses always knew what we needed. That was something I knew to be true. I'd never forget the day after our parents passed, I'd broken down while working with Dolly. She'd given me a gentle nudge and then a good horse hug, offering the comfort I needed in that moment.

"He loves you," I said, shaking my head. "He terrorizes the rest of us."

Sky beamed and then straightened, turning to look around the pasture. "This place is so big."

"It is," I said. "We do a lot with it though. Aside from the rodeo, we offer support for foster children that need a place to feel safe. We also have artist retreats, star gazing, the picnics. I'm grateful for all we get to do with this place."

"It's special," they whispered. "I've never been to a place like it."

*Stay.* I fought saying that aloud, but it still nearly slipped out.

Sometimes, things just felt right. And seeing Sky standing in front of me with the ranch stretching behind them—it felt like they belonged here.

Ma used to say when you know, you know. There were days I felt devastated all over again that we'd lost her and Pa in the same moment, but I knew in my heart that in a way, it'd been a blessing. Those two were never apart, and it would have been a slow death if one of them passed before the other.

That kind of love was why Rainbow Ranch was what it was. The four of us had never struggled the way other people do to feel loved. Even being openly queer, we'd never faced questions from loved ones. I'd never forget when Boone came out—of course, I'd already known. I was his twin. Just like he'd known about me, too.

I rubbed the ache in my chest absentmindedly.

"It looks like the weather for the next couple days will be fully clear in the area," Sky said. "So I can help Pris out and earn my keep."

"I'm sure she'd appreciate the help. Winnie and Boone sometimes lend her a hand when they're able to, but she keeps that part of our ranch going. Between the crops and the garden, she's got everything down to a science. Smarter than all of us put together, I swear."

"I believe it," Sky said.

"Let me show you a couple other things," I said. "Then I'll deliver you to her."

Sky nodded eagerly and I nodded my head to the fence.

"We can go through the gate this time," I said.

"You mean you don't want to manhandle me again?" they teased.

I could feel the blush creeping everywhere. "Sorry about that, I didn't mean to make you uncomfortable or—"

"You didn't," they said quickly. "I liked it, Beau."

Before I could get another word in, they went to the fence, climbed it with ease, and hopped down to the other side. They tossed a wink over their shoulder— and damn, if I wasn't already a goner.

Twenty-four hours. I'd known Sky for twenty-four hours and I felt like I was tumblin' straight into a canyon of desire.

Dennis snorted, looking up at me like he *knew* what I was thinking.

"Shush," I mumbled, shaking my head as I hopped the fence.

"Alright, cowboy," Sky said. "Where to next? Oh, I meant to ask—should I move my van somewhere?"

"We can move it to the garage if you want. That's where I park the truck."

We fell into step next to each other and I matched my strides with theirs. My legs were a lot longer, so we ended up in an easy walk on the gravel road past the horse barn, then the regular barn, until we came to another fence. This one had a gate though, and I unlatched it, the metal screeching on its hinges as we went through.

"We're having a bonfire tonight," I said. "If you want to join us. I think Boone is whipping up s'mores."

"That sounds wonderful," Sky said.

A comfortable silence settled between us as we made our way to the roundabout in front of the house. The van sat there, with the keys still inside.

"Want to see it?" Sky asked.

I had to admit, I was curious. The van was like something out of the *Twisters* movie.

"Sure," I said.

Sky opened up the side door, revealing the inside. I leaned in, humming as I took in the equipment. "I trust everyone on this ranch with my life, but we probably should have put this in the garage yesterday," I winced. "Some of this looks pricey."

"Some of it is," Sky said. "Most of it is photography equipment."

"How long have you been doing this?" I asked.

"About three years," they said. "I got out of college and hit the road."

"Is it rude to ask how old you are?" I asked.

Sky snorted. "Maybe, but I don't care. I'm twenty-six. You?"

"Thirty-five . . ."

They wiggled their brows. "An older man."

I shook my head and braced my hand on the top of the van, leaning against it. "You're trouble, aren't you?"

The corner of their mouth tugged. "Maybe sometimes."

Maybe *all* the time.

"Well," I mumbled. "Let's get the van moved, and I'll show you the garden. I'm sure Pris is already over there."

Sky nodded. "Sounds like a plan to me."

# 5
# sky

THERE WAS something sexy about a woman who knew her way around a tractor. In fact, I was pretty sure Pris was awakening something deep inside me.

I swallowed hard as I leaned against the fence next to Beau, the two of us waiting patiently as she turned it off, hopped out, and walked over to us. She was wearing jeans, boots, a button down denim shirt, and a cowgirl hat—her appearance mirroring Beau's.

Over the last day, I'd discovered I really had a thing for denim shirts.

The tension between these two was something else. The longer I was here, the more I saw it. But, I was pretty sure both of them had yet to broach whatever *this* was.

It wasn't my business, really, but I also liked them too much for my own good. So of course, I wanted to see them happy. And then being a polyamorous romantic, I very much wanted to see them together.

Beau cleared his throat. "Howdy."

She quirked a brow and rested her elbows on the fence. "Howdy." Her warm gaze slid to me and I felt myself blush.

I was starting to accept the fact that I'd permanently be flustered in their presence. "Here to learn how to ride a tractor? Or ride a cowboy?"

Beau choked on air. I fought a laugh, although I felt like I was going to melt straight into the dirt like a popsicle in the sun. "Both?"

Pris' laugh was like sunshine. "Mmhmm. I'm wrapping up here so we can go to the garden. We have some veggies we can pick, and you can take them to Boone and Winnie."

"More than happy to be useful," I said.

"Well, when a storm comes around, you can take me with you," Pris said. "I've always wanted to try storm chasing."

"Really?"

"I don't know about that," Beau mumbled. "Isn't it dangerous?"

"Well, I'd be with a pro," Pris countered, her brows drawing together in annoyance. "Besides, you aren't my boss in my free time."

His ears looked like they'd been sunburned. "Just want you to be safe, is all."

Was I intruding? It damn sure seemed like it.

Pris leaned back from the fence and crossed her arms in front of her chest. "When have I not been safe, Beau Adams? I can take care of myself."

He held up his callused hands. "Never said you couldn't."

Pris narrowed her eyes. "Maybe just say you'd worry about me, then. Instead of being a bossy man."

"I always worry about you, Priscilla," he snapped.

"Well, don't."

He blew out a sharp breath. "Impossible. I'm going back to work. Take care of Sky, will you?"

"Oh, I certainly will."

I winced as Beau walked off, shaking his head as he headed back for the house. Pris let out a heavy sigh.

"Damn it," she mumbled. "Sorry. I just hate it when he does that. He tries to mother-hen all of us, but he doesn't need to do that with me."

"Seems like he just cares," I said softly.

"He cares too much." She made a face and then rolled her shoulders. "He does too much for everyone and then never takes care of himself. It drives me nuts."

I glanced back at him as he stomped inside the house, the screen door snapping shut. "Well . . . I don't know what to say. But of course I'll take you storm chasing if we get the chance to. The weather looks like it'll be clear the next few days."

Pris snorted. "Well, if the weather changes—which we both know it will—plan to have a third. I think he'll have a heart attack if he isn't there too."

I smiled and shrugged. "I don't mind being looked after. Better than being treated like I don't exist."

She hummed and tipped her head back, looking up at the cloudless sky as she mulled that over. "Damn," she mumbled, kicking the dirt before looking at me again. "I know exactly what you mean. I know he does it from a place of caring. It just drives me a little crazy, you know?"

I nodded. "I understand."

Pris offered a smile and then glanced over her shoulder at the piece of equipment sitting there. "Anyway . . . Want to ride the tractor?"

"Uh, yes. Of course," I snorted.

"Great. Don't mind sitting on my lap, do you?"

My mouth dropped. "I . . . I don't mind."

"Great. Hop over."

Only the third time jumping a fence in my life, and this time it was to sit on a gorgeous woman's lap while we rode a tractor.

It was possibly the gayest thing I'd ever done.

I went over the fence, landing softly in the dirt. I rubbed my hands on my thighs and swallowed hard as Pris smirked. She held out her hand, and I took it, letting her lead me over to the tractor.

It was big and green and looked important, which made me nervous. But she opened up the door to the windowed cabin and climbed up with ease, taking a seat and then holding her hand out. I took it and she pulled me up like I weighed no more than a feather.

My cheeks burned as I settled on her lap, becoming all too aware of the way our bodies fit together. It was a tight squeeze with us both in the closed-in space.

"Are you sure this is okay?" I mumbled.

"Yep," she chuckled, shutting the door.

"Okay," I whispered.

I was really sitting on her lap. One arm looped around my waist, holding me tight against her as she reached around with the other and turned the tractor on. It came roaring to life, the entire world rumbling around us.

"What are we harvesting?" I asked over the thrum of the engine.

"Winter wheat," she called. "We'll do a couple rows and head back inside for lunch, or else Boone will track us down."

All I could do was nod, a yelp leaving me as the tractor lurched forward. I squeezed my thighs together, realizing that this definitely did it for me. Every second I spent with Pris was another second I felt like I was going to implode. It didn't help that the vibrations rolling through us felt good.

*Behave yourself.* I repeated that to myself over and over again as we crept forward, the machine mowing down the stalks and harvesting the wheat. I twisted slightly, glancing behind us as I tried to understand how the machine worked.

I caught Pris' smirk and another wink, and twisted back around to face the front.

*I'm a goner.*

———

My legs were wobbly as we walked up the front steps to the house, and I was pretty sure I was wetter than a god damned river between my thighs. I followed Priscilla inside, thinking about the fact that I'd made it out of that without embarrassing myself *too* much.

Would it be bad if I grabbed lunch and then hightailed it back to my room for a little personal TLC?

"I think we're having sandwiches," Pris said as we entered the dining room.

She was right. It looked like Boone had made sandwiches, wrapped in foil and easy to grab in a pile at the center of the table. Next to the sandwiches was a giant, chilled bowl of fresh salad, a mix of brightly colored vegetables that made my mouth water.

I hadn't realized how hungry I was until now, but lusting after Pris and Beau worked up an appetite. A few Gatorades waited there too, cold and sweating from the warmth of the day.

My chest squeezed as I realized Beau was nowhere to be seen.

He had every right to be worried about Pris if she came storm chasing with me. I was mostly used to the adrenaline and danger of it, but it was still risky. Tornadoes were devastating forces of nature, and in my pursuit to help the world understand them better, I put my life at risk.

"Howdy," Benny said, giving me a wave. "Saw that you met Dennis."

"I did." I grinned, looping my thumbs in my jeans. "He's so sweet."

Billie was seated at the head of the table and let out a low laugh. "Sweet? I guess he can be. He keeps all of us on our toes."

"I can see that," I chuckled. "How long has he been at Rainbow Ranch?"

"Ohh, hmmm. . ." Billie trailed off with a frown, looking up at Benny. "A couple years? Right?"

"I think so," he said. "Seems like forever. He definitely belongs here. Our own little mascot at this point."

"He's so cute at the rodeo," Pris said.

"I bet he is." I grabbed a plate, a sandwich, and a bit of fresh salad that was on the table. While I still wanted to escape to my room for *reasons*, I was enjoying the conversation too much to leave. "This salad looks so good."

"Pris grew all of that," Boone said as he swung through the room. He was wearing an apron, a smudge of flour on his cheek. He nodded toward the gorgeous greens, tomatoes, and peppers as he put down a plate of the biggest chocolate chip cookies I'd ever seen.

"Really?" I looked over at Pris as she settled down in a chair. "Also, I need one of those cookies."

Boone grinned. "They're the best of the best."

"Yes, and please grab me one before the vultures descend," she said.

I plucked two off the plate before everyone else could grab them and laughed as I settled next to her, putting it on her plate. The chocolate chips were still a little gooey, and I put my cookie down and then licked some off my fingertips.

"Farm-to-table, baby," Boone said, coming around the table to give her a hug around the shoulders. She leaned back into him, grinning from ear to ear. "We take that very seriously around here. I don't know what I'd do without you, Pris."

"Be a sad cook," Billie chuckled.

We all laughed and Pris pecked his cheek. "Thanks for lunch, Boone. Now, if you can just get your brother to be a little more like you . . ."

Boone snorted as he stood up, planting a hand on his hip. "Oh god. What happened now?"

"Nothing." Her gaze flicked to me. "He's just stubborn, is all."

"Well, that ain't new," Benny said. "But we love him for it."

Everyone agreed, and some of the tension in Pris seemed to melt.

"Yeah," she sighed. "We sure do."

# 6
# priscilla

STARS DANCED above us in a clear night sky, only interrupted by the burning glow of the bonfire. It was a chilly evening, the warmth of the day long receded. Camp chairs were sprawled around and there were even a couple of picnic blankets spread on the grass.

Nothing could beat bonfires on nights like this. Not a single cloud in the sky, it was as if we were looking up at the universe. It made me feel so small and so big all at the same time.

My muscles felt nice and worked from the long work day.

What *didn't* feel good was the fact that I'd been lusting over Sky ever since they sat on my lap in the tractor. Well, okay, that felt good too, but it also was bad news.

I couldn't get them out of my head.

No matter what I did.

It didn't help that they were in my space for the rest of the day. We had lunch together, and then they helped me in the garden for a while—we were side by side for hours on end.

I was learning about them, and everything I learned, I liked. Like how they'd been storm chasing for a couple of years, and they were a photographer, and they loved to help people. They came out as nonbinary a few years ago, and it'd been a struggle at first, but they'd found themself. They'd fought for themself.

I had nothing but pure admiration for them. I knew how hard it was to advocate for yourself, especially if you were raised to be a people pleaser.

Then there was the Beau problem.

All day, I could practically hear that damn man grumbling from his office, despite the fact that the doors were closed. It didn't matter what part of the ranch we were on, I could feel that man stewing from a mile away.

Without fail, he always managed to drive me just a little bit crazy. I knew that he was coming from a good place earlier in regards to the storm chasing, but it wasn't like I'd be going out to do it alone. And yes, of course we all knew it was dangerous, but that didn't mean that I didn't want to try it out with Sky.

*They* were the professional here.

Then there was the fact I could see he was worried about them going out, too.

He wouldn't admit that, though. At least not yet. But it was painted all over his ruggedly handsome face.

The tension I felt with Sky was the same tension I felt with him.

Different, but the same.

And I knew with just one look he was feeling that tension with them, too. It was clear as day Beau had a soft spot for our storm-chasing stranger.

I tugged the patchwork quilt around my shoulders. The fabric was soft and worn, each patch telling a story. I knew it was one of the blankets that'd been around this ranch for years, and it carried that familiarity with it.

My face was warm, the fire emanating heat in comforting waves. Occasionally it would pop, and sparks would float up toward the stars.

Bonfire nights were always my favorite. We usually did it about once a week, and Boone always made the best s'mores.

It also gave us all the time to connect with each other in a different way. We weren't working right now, and all of our worries were put aside.

Sometimes, when we had guests on the ranch, it would be a big production. But tonight, it was just our close-knit group, plus Sky.

They sat across from me in a camp chair, a blanket wrapped around their shoulders. It was one that Mama Adams had made long ago too, and it made me smile thinking about her now.

I'd never forget when she and Mr. Adams passed away. Even though I'd already been away from Rainbow Ranch and out in the world at the time, I'd still heard about it, and it broke my heart into a million pieces.

Those two had made such a large impact on my life as a teenager, and I never really had the chance to tell them.

It made sense that I'd come back here. Not that I owed anyone anything, but that this place had always felt like home. And it was my time here that made me want to pursue a degree in agriculture. Working with the earth and bringing my expertise in soil sciences and environmental sustainability to the ranch, working with people, creating a safe place—all of those things brought me joy and peace.

It made me feel like I was contributing to the world in a meaningful way.

And for that, we could all thank Mr. and Mrs. Adams for the love that they had for their kids while they were growing up.

I'd zoned out, but as I blinked and came back to the present, soft laughter floated on the breeze. Wiley and Boone were tucked against each other, snuggling as they roasted s'mores. Benny was drinking a beer and looking through a telescope up at the stars, and Billie was playing a game with Winnie.

Then there was Beau.

Our lone cowboy stood just a few feet away from me, his arms crossed as he watched the fire. He occasionally let out a sigh, and even though he wasn't a father, it was definitely a *dad* sigh.

Because of course he was the one that was keeping track of the wind, keeping an eye on everyone, making sure all of us were safe.

The man never took a break. I couldn't say I took breaks very often either , but I still knew how to relax.

The sound of boots scuffing over rocks made me turn my head. Beau looked up at me, made a face, and then apparently made the decision that he was going to talk to me.

"Can I sit?" he asked.

"Yeah," I said.

He settled down in the empty chair next to me.

I sighed dramatically, giving him the look. "Did you decide to apologize to me?"

He snorted, but took off his hat, resting it on his knee. "I just want you to be safe. I care about you, Priscilla."

"I know you do. But that doesn't mean you get to make decisions for me. And it wasn't even that serious."

"But I know you," he protested. "I know that you would

go storm chasing. After seeing how powerful that tornado was yesterday morning, the idea of you and Sky getting swept away in that . . . I can't bear the thought of it, Pris. It scares the shit out of me."

My chest ached. "You mean, what would you do if we got into trouble and you couldn't be there to save us?"

He wrinkled his nose, but didn't argue. He didn't argue because he knew I was right.

"Listen," I breathed out. "I know that when you talk like that, you're coming from a good place. But we've known each other for a very long time. By now, don't you think I know how to handle myself?"

"It's not a matter of handling yourself," he said gently. "You can handle anything in the world, darlin', but a tornado is a force none of us can fight. I know storm chasing means you're chasing it, not the other way around, but you know how fast things can change."

"And what about Sky? It's their profession. Are you going to give them the same lecture?"

He didn't say anything, but he looked up at them. The firelight flickered, casting a warm glow on his jaw and sharp cheekbones, dancing in his softening eyes. The way he looked at them made my heart skip a beat.

God, how many times had I dreamed of him looking at me that way? Countless.

For a moment, I wondered why we'd never crossed that line. I wasn't stupid. I knew there was tension between us. But neither one of us had ever dared to pass it.

"I don't know what to say," he murmured. "We've just met them."

"Yeah, but I have eyes," I muttered. "I see the way you look at them. They're going to be gone in the blink of an eye, you know?"

His shoulders deflated on a heavy sigh. "I know. Don't you worry about anything with that. But, to answer your question, I don't like the idea of Sky storm chasing alone either. It sounds like they had an assistant, and they had a falling out. So now they've been doing this alone in a state that isn't very friendly to any of us. Storm chasing is dangerous. We all know how unpredictable the weather could be. So yeah, maybe I'll end up giving them the same lecture too, even though they barely know me."

"Your big heart must be a heavy burden, Beau Adams," I said.

Beau leaned over, surprising me by resting his hand on my knee. He gave me a gentle squeeze, and then drew back to stand.

Even though there was a fire burning right in front of us, it felt like he took the warmth away with his touch.

"I'm sorry for upsetting you," he said. "You know I trust you. You know I believe in your instincts. You know I think the world of you. And you know it'd break me if something ever happened to you."

My eyes widened in surprise. I opened my mouth to speak, but no words came out. He placed his hat back on top of his head, and then strolled over to his sister and Winnie. They were playing a game of poker, and within a few seconds, he'd been folded in.

Well, damn. I was speechless. What the hell did he mean by that?

I shook my head and stood up to stretch my legs. I wandered around the fire to where Boone and Wylie were snuggled up.

"Look at you two," I said. "All damn cozy."

Boone grinned. "Want a s'more?"

"Of course I do," I said.

He lifted a plate, offering me a skewer with a marshmallow on it.

"How about you take one to your *friend*?" Wylie asked, wiggling his brows.

Boone's brows shot up. "Oh? *Oh*."

"Shush," I muttered, but I took a second skewer and marshmallow. "Mind your business, both of you."

That earned a few mischievous giggles as I turned and walked over to Sky. They looked up at me with a smile as I offered it to them.

"Thanks," they said. "Can't remember the last time I've had one of these."

"Oh yes. It's been far too long since I've had a good s'more. And by too long, I mean it's been a week. Boone's homemade graham crackers with the melty chocolate are always the best."

Sky laughed as they took the skewer and scooted their chair forward. We both leaned in, casting our marshmallows over the open flames.

"So, bonfires once a week?" Sky asked.

"Usually," I said. "In the summer, we'll do more than one a week. Especially if we have guests. There are times we'll host retreats or have picnics, like the Y'all Pride Picnic coming up. People like to visit this place."

"Of course they do," Sky said. "I've only ever heard good things."

The marshmallows started to bubble on the outside as they heated. I always liked mine a little burnt and crispy.

"I think most of us only have good things to say," I said. "And of course, sometimes we end up keeping people. Plenty of room to have people live here full-time . . ."

*What on earth am I doing?* I was basically telling Sky they could stay.

45

And they could, of course. But normally, that wasn't something I ever brought up.

But maybe . . .

*Maybe* I liked the idea of them staying.

"That's good to know," they said.

I swallowed hard as Sky pulled their marshmallow back. They stood up, and we carried our now charred fluff to where Boone waited. Wylie chuckled at his boyfriend as he clasped my marshmallow between two graham crackers, and a wedge of chocolate. It started to melt, smashing together in a delicious little sandwich.

"Look at that," Boone said. "Perfection."

I pulled it off the skewer, watching as Sky did the same thing.

More than anything else, I wanted to see their face as they took the first bite.

I waited, smiling as they bit into it.

And of course, their expression was the biggest reward. Maybe even better than the marshmallow concoction itself. I bit into mine, letting out a hum of satisfaction.

"Oh my god," Sky groaned. "These are amazing. What's your secret, Boone?"

Boone grinned from ear to ear. "Oh, you know. Fresh graham crackers are always easy to make. I make the best ones. Mama's recipe, of course. And then the chocolate is a secret."

"I know what they are," Wylie said. "He tells me all of his secrets. They're—"

Boone clasped his hand over Wylie's mouth. "Not so fast there, cowboy," he said. "Can't just go handing out my secret secrets like that."

Wylie smirked, and we all knew that he wasn't actually going to tell us the secret. But it was still funny, and I shook my head at the two of them, amused by their cuteness.

Sky and I retreated back to the camp chairs and sat down next to each other. I looked over at them, unable to keep myself from drinking in the way they glowed in the firelight. A bit of chocolate sat on the corner of their mouth and I leaned over.

"You've got a little . . ."

They looked at me, blushing as I swiped the chocolate away with my thumb.

"Thanks," they whispered.

I licked it away, my heart pounding. I felt eyes on the two of us and glanced up.

Beau was watching us, his expression unreadable.

Sky cleared their throat, Beau looked away, and I felt like I was going to faint from the tension in the air. I wasn't sure anyone else felt it like we did, though. *What is happening here?*

I decided to try to be normal. "How are you feeling?" I asked.

"Oh, good," they said. "A little sore. Certainly doing what we did today is different than me being hunched over in a car. Or having the posture of a shrimp over my laptop."

I snorted. "Definitely a lot different."

"I was just thinking, though . . . I kind of want to take pictures of the farm. Pictures of people in action, in your daily lives. It's different than storm chasing, that's for sure. But I have the camera here, and they could always be used for the website."

"That's not a bad idea," I said. "I'm sure it would be appreciated. You just have to make sure you get my good side."

"Pris, you don't have a bad side."

I laughed and took another bite of my s'more. Everything felt a little bit brighter right now. Between the sound of the fire crackling, people chattering, and the occasional stray howl or snort from a horse . . .

Everything was perfect.

I had to admit it—there was something that felt right about sitting next to Sky. I couldn't let myself think that way though. They'd be leaving soon enough.

Nevermind having them sit on my lap at the tractor was one of the hottest things I've ever done.

On that thought, it was time to go to bed. Not to sleep—it was time to get my vibrator and work out some of the sexual frustration I felt from today. I licked the leftover chocolate and marshmallow off my fingers, and then stood up.

"I'm hittin' the hay," I said. "Need any help getting back to your room?"

Oh god, that sounded like an invitation. Sky shook their head, though, taking it the way I had meant it.

"I think I should be able to find my way. Thank you for today, Pris. Especially for that tractor ride."

That tractor ride would be exactly what I was thinking about as I pleased myself. I winked at them, and then turned on my boots, waving my hand.

"Good night, everyone," I called.

Everyone wished me good night and I made my way back to the house, stepping into the quiet. I breathed out slowly, savoring the moment. It was rare to be the only person in the house. The wood creaked underfoot down the hall to my bedroom. I slipped inside and shut the door.

Everyone else would be up for a while, which meant I could have the bathroom to myself for just a little bit. I quickly gathered up my things, and then carried them back down the hall to the shower.

Locking myself in, I flipped on the hot water and stripped. I gathered my curls and slid on my shower cap. There was no need for a washday today and I was glad, because the deep conditioning alone took forever.

It felt good to be out of my clothes and away from everyone. I stepped into the shower, tugging the curtain closed. Steam swirled around my body as I ran my hands up and down.

Already, my thoughts turned back to Sky.

It was just a fantasy—one I had no business having. But I didn't stop myself. Because it was just that, a *fantasy*.

A fantasy, never hurt anyone, did it?

The hot water relaxed my muscles as my fingertips slid down to my pussy. I sucked in a breath, stifling a moan as I circled my clit, dipping further down and realizing just how wet I was.

Damn that tractor ride. Having them sit on my lap had been the best worst idea of the century. Their sweet scent and the softness of them lingered in my mind.

I could still feel the sunshine on my skin and blazing heat creeping up my spine. I covered my mouth to stifle any sounds I might make as I circled faster.

A soft groan left me, and I thought about what it would be like to be with both Sky and Beau.

"Damn it," I rasped.

I had no business thinking about the two of them together, but I'd seen how Beau looked at them. I'd seen it, and it'd sparked something in me.

I knew both of them would take direction well.

The idea of having two submissives at the same time . . .

Or even making Beau do things to Sky, instructing him on how to touch them . . .

*That* would be the perfect situation.

"Fuck," I mumbled.

Not to mention, all the kinky things we could do together.

The saying that three was a crowd got it all wrong when it came to kink and love. Not that I was in love with either one of them . . .

I circled my clit faster, pleasure rushing through my body. My heart pounded as I got closer and closer, all of my thoughts and fantasies building up until I felt the pressure rolling down my spine.

I was so close. So damn close.

My imagination was far too vivid for my own good. I thought about Beau—our strong, stubborn, sweet cowboy. And then I thought about Sky—our charming, brave, shy storm chaser.

I *needed* them.

The very thought of being with those two together sent me over the edge, my toes curling as my orgasm rushed through me. Shock waves sparked across my skin, and I rode out the high of it until I collapsed against the wall, breathing hard.

I needed that relief.

I stayed like that for a few seconds, catching my breath. Letting myself enjoy the euphoric cloud that followed after coming so hard.

"Just a fantasy," I whispered to myself.

But it would be a dream come true if it were real.

# 7
# beau

IT'D BEEN a week since the storm had brought Sky to our doorstep, and I was certain that I'd never wanted anyone more.

Well...

Except for the person I *couldn't* have.

Priscilla stood outside in the garden working with Sky, showing them the ropes. For all the storms we'd had over the last couple weeks, there were moments like this where sunshine was like a thousand crushed diamonds haloing the ranch in its sparkly warmth.

From my office, I could see a good bit. The stables, the garden, the compost, the fields that stretched in the distance with our crops. My office itself was simple but functional. Rustic and reminiscent of how Pa had it, although I'd changed a few things around. What had stayed the same for as long as I could remember was the faded yellow landline phone that sat on the edge of the wooden desk, the stacks of notebooks and papers that covered everything else, and the pictures on the walls. Faded photographs of the ranch, our family. Pictures of when Boone and I were kids, or of Benny and Billie from when they were babies.

Occasionally, I'd catch a whiff of Pa's cologne or Ma's perfume, as if they'd melted into the wooden floors to stay. Ghosts of two people I missed every single day.

Seven years. It'd been seven years since the wreck. Seven years since the four of us lost our parents and inherited an entire ranch to run.

Seven years since I'd taken the reins and had become the one who always had the answers.

I was disassociating again. I raked my fingers through my hair and tore my gaze away from Pris and Sky, only for it to immediately wander back. Pris was standing next to them, her hand settling on Sky's lower back in a way that had my brows raising.

Suddenly, I felt very thirsty. Parched, even.

Dammit. I needed to focus on work. I needed to get my thoughts back in order. There was so much planning to do, and we were hosting the Y'all Pride Picnic this weekend. Fingers crossed we didn't have any other tornadoes blow through. For the most part, everything was ready to go for that, but we'd be up at the crack of dawn on Saturday morning to set up a few tents, roll out blankets, and set up tables. It would be a lot of work, but we all pulled together easily. Right now, it was looking like we'd have about two-hundred people coming to the ranch, and all the money raised would help a charity to support trans youth in Oklahoma.

I checked my emails quickly, rubbing my temples as I read one from Doc Evans, the veterinarian out of Johnson Springs. We'd known Doc for years and had a good deal with him. He gave us a break on medical expenses for our horses, and we helped him out with some of the rougher cases he saw.

Such as Noodles, a blood bay gelding who Wylie was working magic with. He'd come out of a bad hoarding situation outside of Stillwater, and when he'd first come to the ranch, he'd been so incredibly wary of humans that it hurt to see. But slowly, we were gaining his trust. It would take months, if not years, to get him to where we wanted—but the progress we were already seeing was incredible.

Doc's email was just a recap of the expenses from Noodles' little cake eating adventure a few weeks ago. I winced when I saw the numbers, but we'd make it work. We always made it work.

A knock at the door startled me. My head whipped up, and I was surprised to see Billie standing there. Normally, she was out with the horses at this time of day.

"Abilene," I greeted, chuckling as her nose scrunched.

"Why you gotta use my full name like that?"

"Because you're my little sister," I said. "I have to do that, or else the world tips out of balance."

She grinned, but then something flickered in her brown eyes. I frowned in response.

"What's wrong?" I asked immediately.

"Nothing," she said. "Well . . . I just noticed that Pris and Sky seem to be getting cozy."

My brows shot up. It took every ounce of control not to look back at the two of them again.

Given that Billie and I had known each other all of her life, it was difficult to disguise my expression. I shrugged. "And?"

She narrowed her eyes on me. "And? I thought you and Pris were gonna be a thing. You've had eyes on her for years."

Dammit. Why did Billie have to be so observant? "I don't know what you're talking about," I said, reaching for a stack of papers to . . . restack. Casually. Shuffling them. "Pris is a gorgeous, smart, talented woman."

"Yep. And you're a kind, hardworking, handsome man. Although, maybe *handsome* is sort of a stretch."

I gave her the *look*. "And?"

"And? I'm not blind. I've also seen you looking at Sky over the last week. Every night at dinner. Every morning at breakfast. Lunch, even. I really like them, by the way. They're very sweet."

They were sweeter than Ma's honey peach tea. I'd yet to spend much time with them alone, but every encounter always left me yearning for more. And dammit, Billie was right. I had been looking at them at all our meals.

I thought no one would notice.

Apparently, I was wrong.

Pris had noticed too. But I'd noticed the way she looked at them, too. . .

It made me wonder what would happen if the three of us . . .

*Stop*.

I cleared my throat. "Billie, since when do you get involved in other people's business like this? You know better."

"Well, you're my brother."

"Oldest brother," I quipped.

She snorted. "Sure. And Boone is so happy with Wylie. I think we'd all like to see you happy, too."

"I *am* happy," I protested.

"Oh yeah? Is that why you've stacked those papers ten times and won't look me in the eye?"

I looked up at her and glared. "I'm happy. And besides,

falling in love with someone isn't the only way to be happy. We can all be happy alone. Single. I get plenty of joy from everything I do."

"Okay." She held up her hands in mock defense. "I'm just saying, Pris deserves love too. So does Sky. Could be the perfect situation."

It *could* be, but it wouldn't be.

"Sky will be gone before we know it," I said. "And we've known Pris for years. If something was gonna happen there, it probably would have happened by now, don't you think?"

Billie shrugged. "Knowing how you drag your feet when it comes to personal matters, not really."

"*Abilene Anne*," I growled.

She batted her eyelashes. "See you at dinner, *Boss*."

My ears were burning as she left me alone to stew. What was it about my siblings? Always interfering and gettin' in business they shouldn't be in.

Although I wasn't any different, was I? I'd spotted how Boone and Wylie looked at each other right from the start, which was why I'd talked to Wylie. Warned him that if he did anything to hurt Boone, there'd be trouble.

Of course, those two had quickly fallen head over boot, and Wylie was a great guy. Things worked out.

We always watched out for each other. It was impossible not to. I knew Billie would only mention something if she was worried about me.

The thing was, I thought I was hiding my secret desires a little better than that.

But, if Billie was mentioning it to me, that meant I wasn't hiding my desires well *at all*. It also meant that other people were probably picking up on it, as well.

The last thing that I wanted was to make Pris or Sky feel uncomfortable. Especially with the position I was in, being the one who ran the ranch. And also being a man. I recognized the privilege I had and with the power dynamics too, I just didn't want to ever do anything to cause harm to the people I cared about.

But I'd be a damn liar if I didn't admit that I've been thinking about the two of them.

It'd been a long time since I let my desires run free.

Sky was the spark, but now the two of them were a wildfire spreading across my heart. My cock stirred as a thought of being with them both, of getting on my knees to worship their bodies.

I knew Pris would be the one to take control. While we'd never talked in depth about sex or BDSM, we'd touched on the topic here and there over the years and she'd told me she enjoyed Domming. There were nights I'd lay awake wondering what it would be like to be with her. I'd never had a partner who wanted to take the reins, but I was a switch, and there was a first time for everything. I trusted Priscilla explicitly, too.

If ever given the chance to be with her, I'd kneel for her in a heartbeat.

But what about Sky?

Based on my interactions with them, if I had to guess, I'd say that they were more submissive behind closed doors.

More than anything, I wished I could explore those parts of ourselves with each other. Exploring kink and BDSM was something I rarely got to do, and I always yearned for those opportunities. They were hard to come by, given where I lived.

Maybe just for tonight, I'd let myself imagine those scenarios all the way through. Please myself, get it out of my system, and move on—going back to the man who didn't daydream about being with two people who would never look at him that way.

I had too much going on, didn't I? Too much going on to be a good partner to anyone.

Pris and Sky deserved a good partner that could give them the whole world.

Someone better than me.

I pushed back from my desk and stood up, rolling my shoulders back and trying to release some of the stress I felt. And of course, I looked back out the window—but this time, Sky and Pris weren't there.

*Where'd they go?*

*Knock, knock.* I spun around and my breath whooshed out.

Sky stood there, a ray of sunshine. Bright smile, bright eyes, even brighter hair.

"Hi," I breathed out.

"Howdy, Beau." They leaned against the door frame. "I wanted to see if I could use the internet in here? I need to get some work done on my laptop if that's okay. I helped out Pris with the garden, and she told me I could go do whatever I needed to do . . ."

"Oh," I said. "Of course. You don't need my permission."

I looked around, suddenly embarrassed by how messy it was in here with all the countless notebooks and papers and pens everywhere over the desktop. There was a spare chair in the corner, and I went to it quickly, hauling it to the desk.

"You don't need to make space for me," they said. "I can always sit on the floor."

"You're not sitting on the floor," I snorted. "I have plenty of space for you."

They let out a soft laugh, and that broke whatever

tension I was feeling. I paused for a second, closing my eyes as I felt a smile emerge.

"Sorry," I drawled. "I'm a little all over the place today. And for whatever reason, when you're in my presence, it makes it even worse."

*Oh.* I'd really just said that.

This time, when I looked up at Sky, they had a different expression on their face. I swallowed hard, wondering if I'd just ruined everything. Probably, right? My tongue felt tied, my heart beating out of my chest.

They took a step toward me. Then another.

One step after the other, until we stood boot to boot, their head tipping back as they looked up.

More than anything, I wanted to kiss them.

"Sky," I croaked.

Heat rolled through me, sweltering and needy. All of those thoughts that'd been swirling around my head came roaring back.

They were so close.

Barely an inch between our bodies.

I swallowed hard, wondering what I was doing. Wondering what they were doing.

"I really like you," they whispered. "I don't know why. I know we just met. But every time I'm around you, I can't think about anything else but kissing you. Is that wrong?"

"No," I said. "It's not wrong at all."

"Then will you kiss me?"

My breath hitched. It was the only thing I could think about. My gaze swept from their sweet eyes to their soft lips. Their eyelashes were long and dark, sunlight catching the tips as it poured in through the window. The office felt like an inferno.

I carefully lifted my hand, sliding it behind their neck.

Their eyes fluttered, a soft moan leaving them that had me melting.

Of course they made the prettiest sounds in the world.

"Are you certain?" I asked.

"Yes," they whispered. "But only if you want to."

"Oh, I want to."

I leaned down, my mind racing as I wondered how long it had been since I'd kissed someone. Too damn long. What if I was bad at it?

All of those thoughts melted away as our lips brushed against each other. They leaned into me, their body soft against mine.

Our kiss was gentle at first.

But then, a lightning strike of desire bolted through us, and our kiss deepened with a raw hunger that'd been haunting me since they tumbled into my life.

Sky leaned up on their tiptoes, winding their arms around my neck.

My hands fell to their hips, and I lifted them with ease, putting them on the desk. Papers and folders flew to the floor, making a mess around us.

None of that mattered.

The only thing that mattered was them, their kiss, the feel of their body against mine. The pleasure pumping through me, heavy like a drug.

God, they tasted just as sweet as I'd imagined.

I didn't pull away until we were both breathless. Pink blushed their cheeks, their eyes wide with surprise.

"Was that okay?" I whispered.

"More than," they said.

Their eyes slowly slid from my face down my chest to where the bulge in my jeans had grown. They swallowed hard, reaching up and looping a finger through my belt loop.

"Damn," they whispered.

"Sky," I choked out.

The way they looked at me brought up every protective instinct I had. I wanted to keep them safe, to be with them, and to give them the whole world and more.

"I didn't expect to come in here and kiss you," they said. "But I'm glad I did."

"Me too," I said.

"What are you doing tonight?" they whispered.

"I don't have any plans after dinner. I usually come back here to work."

"Does anyone ever bother you in the office?"

A slow smile crept over. "Not *typically*."

Sky grinned. "Maybe I can come work with you."

"I'd like that, Sky."

I couldn't help it. I leaned down again, brushing my lips against theirs. They held me there, the kiss deepening all over again, the sparks flying. I grunted, desperate for more.

Something had changed. Something was stirred up inside me now, and I couldn't turn away. If it weren't the middle of the day, I'd be keen on shutting the door, locking it, and taking them right here on the desk.

A throat cleared, and I damn near launched myself across the room away from Sky. I looked up, my chest, squeezing as I saw Priscilla.

"Pris," I said, breathing out.

"Sorry," she said. "I . . . wasn't trying to interrupt."

Her gaze lingered on me and then slowly slid over to Sky. And then she left, the sound of her boots quickly fading.

Fuck. Another feeling rose up, and I wasn't really sure what it was.

Worry? Sadness? Both?

Sky crossed their arms over their chest, their expression twisting. "Can I ask you something?"

"Of course."

"Are you and Pris a thing?"

"No . . ." Although everyone seemed to think so today.

"Do you want to be?"

Well, that was the question of the century, wasn't it?

Of course I wanted to be. But I worried about not being enough. Plus, Pris was always here and if I fucked up, I'd never forgive myself.

"Yes," I finally admitted. "But I doubt she wants me. And we've never been together, never even talked about it."

Sky slid off the desk and put their hand on my chest. "I think you should talk to her. I think you might be surprised by what you hear. And I'd like to just say . . . I'm interested in her, too."

"That doesn't bother me," I whispered. "Sky . . . I don't . . . I'm not sure what to say right now."

"How about I'll see you tonight?"

"What about your computer work?"

"I'll do that tomorrow," they said. "I want to go talk to Pris, given that she just walked in on us kissing."

All I could do was nod, completely speechless as they left the office.

A storm was brewing between the three of us.

I just hoped we'd still be standing at the end of it.

# 8
# sky

Kissing Beau was just as amazing as I thought it would be.

And I was already causing trouble in a place that was being so kind to me.

Over the last week, Rainbow Ranch had started to feel like a home. I had to keep reminding myself that I was leaving in just a couple weeks. All of this would soon be behind me . . .

So might as well make the best of it, right?

Like kissing the really hot cowboy?

I don't know what came over me in the office, but for that moment, I'd lost all my worries about being too much. And damn, that kiss.

*That kiss* had completely swept me away.

But then Pris had walked in on us.

Had I ruined everything?

I hadn't expected to walk in and kiss Beau, but the pull had been too magnetic. It was the same pull I felt to her though, which left me feeling confused and worried that I was going to cause problems.

Seven days. Seven days of basking in the tension between the three of us.

I'd found a good routine and I enjoyed helping out Pris. So far the weather hasn't been bad, mostly clear within the area. I'd been able to take some time to go through all the photographs I've taken over the last few weeks, and get everything sorted in the way that I wanted to.

I also had time to check up on my ex-assistant's social media accounts, to see what they were saying online. So far, nothing bad.

The storm chasing world was small. The last thing I wanted was to have a bad reputation. Especially since I was trying to do good, honest work. I was trying to help people.

All of those thoughts fell to the wayside as I found Pris in her room across from mine. The door was wide open. She sat on her bed, her cowgirl hat balanced on her denim-clad knee. She was wearing a denim shirt with a red bandana, her deep brown curls pulled back into a ponytail. Pris was as gorgeous as ever, always managing to steal my breath anytime I laid eyes on her.

I hesitated, and then knocked on the door frame.

She looked up, her brows raising slightly in surprise. "I thought you'd still be with Beau."

"I didn't plan for that to happen," I said quickly. "I didn't plan to walk in and kiss him—"

"You don't need to explain yourself to me," she said, shrugging her shoulders.

Despite her shrug, the tension in the room was thick.

"Can I come in?" I whispered.

Pris nodded, and I crossed from the threshold to the foot of her bed.

I was going to be brave about this. After everything I'd

lost in my life, I was going to go after what I wanted, no matter how fleeting it was. *Be brave. Be strong.*

"Am I imagining things? Is there not something here between us?" I asked.

Pris' eyes hardened. "You were just kissing Beau and now you're asking me if there's something between us, too?"

I winced, realizing how that must've sounded. My chest ached as I struggled to find the right words. "I didn't mean for that to come across that way. I don't know what it is, but there's something about you and there's something about Beau, too. I want both of you, Pris, but I shouldn't have made the assumption that both of you were interested in me as well."

Her expression softened. "Well, for the record, I *am* polyamorous. Although, I've never had the chance to date multiple people at the same time. I'm not sure Beau is, though. Can't say we've ever discussed it. Regardless, you're going to be gone soon. Unless you're planning on staying at Rainbow Ranch?"

I swallowed hard. "I'll be here until storm season is over."

"And then?"

I didn't really want to think about the future at the moment. This was the best and safest I'd felt in a really long time, and I wasn't sure I ever wanted to go home.

Not that I even had a real home. My home had been the van for the last six months.

"I don't really know yet," I admitted. "I'm still figuring things out. Working on the ranch has been tough. It's hard work. I'm not used to being off my phone so much. But, being with you has made it fly by. The bonfires, the way everyone is just here for each other, the horses. It feels special. I've enjoyed spending time with you."

"Sky, I've enjoyed spending time with you," she said gently. "But I also don't really like doing casual relationships. I struggle with it."

"I struggle with it too," I whispered.

In fact, I had a tendency to dive in way too fast. Much to my detriment most of the time. Every time I ended up having my heart broken, I put another tough layer around myself to try to protect it from that hurt.

But then it happened again. And again.

Just like now. Here I was, diving in headfirst. And yet . .
.

"I also know that there are sparks here, and I don't wanna walk away from them," I whispered.

Maybe that wasn't right of me to do since I was planning on leaving. Then again, every time I was around her or Beau, I just wanted more. I wanted to explore my desires, I wanted to explore whatever tension there was between us.

Becoming who I was taught me to embrace all the good moments. It taught me to never let something like this go by without taking it all the way.

The problem was, I often ended up hurting people in the process. And I didn't want to hurt Pris. I didn't want to hurt Beau either.

"I'm sorry," I said. "I don't want to push or anything like that. I'm sorry if I made you feel awkward or if I've disrupted things between you and Beau."

Pris snorted and stood up, grabbing her hat. A few loose curls that laid flat against her head disappeared as she placed her hat on top. She crossed her arms as she looked me up and down.

"Do you always apologize this much?" she asked.

"Well . . . maybe."

"Okay, well, rule number one. Don't apologize to me for

something that doesn't need apologizing for. You didn't do anything wrong. Beau and I are not a couple, and we've never been together. We've never even kissed. We've never once talked about anything like that, and I've known him for years."

Pris sucked in a breath, her shoulders softening before she continued.

"I think if he were interested in me, he would've said something by now. He's known you for just a couple days, and he's already kissed you. And I'm not saying that from a place of jealousy . . . Okay, well maybe I am a little bit jealous of you."

"Jealous of *me*?" I asked in disbelief.

She wrinkled her nose. "Yes. I don't like it, either. Not my favorite feeling. But I feel jealous because I want to kiss you. And I also want to kiss that bossy cowboy. But, I can't do either, because then I'll go falling in love with the both of you. Then you'll leave, and Beau will . . . Well, I don't know what."

I opened my mouth to say something, but my words faltered as she took a step closer, her fingers knotting in my hair at the base of my head. She leaned in, stunning me speechless as she kissed me hard on the lips.

Fireworks burst through me. Kissing her was different than kissing Beau. Both of them were equally amazing. I swooned against her, a whimper leaving me as she took control, stealing my breath until she drew back.

"I'm an idiot," she sighed, her eyes soft and sparkly.

And then she kissed me again.

This time, I leaned up and wrapped my arms around her. Our hips pressed against each other, her fingers knotting in my short hair at the base of my head.

The heat between us was something else. Waves of

need rippled through me, a hunger for something more taking over.

God, I wanted her. I wanted her so damn bad.

This time, when she drew back, she pressed her forehead to mine.

"You're nothing but trouble, Sky," she whispered.

"Hopefully the good kind," I croaked.

She chuckled, and then kissed my cheek. We stood like that for a few seconds. I was in awe of her.

"Pris . . ." I whispered. "What are we doing?"

She shook her head. "Don't know yet, honestly. Don't you need to go get some work done? Some of your storm stuff?"

The subject change was a little jarring. I blew out a breath. "Well, Beau and I kind of left it on a note that I could work in the office tomorrow. I also may have suggested that we see each other tonight . . . But I won't do that if there's something between the two of you. I think you should talk."

"I don't know. I'll think about it. Would you have a problem if we were together? Even though that'll never happen."

"No," I said immediately. "No, it would make me happy if the two of you were."

She shook her head, but she seemed less resistant to the idea of talking to him now.

"We'll see," she said. "For now, maybe take some time to yourself. Or go see if Boone and Winnie need help. Deal?"

I nodded. "Deal."

# 9
# priscilla

AFTER SKY LEFT, I stood in my room, trying to reason with myself. Sunlight poured in, warming the quilt on my bed. I set my hat to the side, spread out, and stared at the ceiling as my mind spiraled.

That kiss had been something else. That kiss had awakened a deep, deep longing inside of me, going against all the rules I'd set for myself. I told myself I wouldn't kiss them, I wouldn't pursue them. And yet, here I was doing the exact thing I said I wouldn't. It certainly didn't help that I'd spent time getting to know them this entire week. And because of it, I'd had more than a few sessions with myself to satiate the lust they had drawn up.

Why couldn't these things be easy? Why couldn't relationships always work out?

At the end of the day, underneath the strong exterior I built, I was still a hopeless romantic. I still yearned to be loved, to be wanted. I yearned to be taken care of. And after spending years with someone who never appreciated me the way I should've been, it'd been so much easier to lock my heart inside a bullpen than to pursue anyone who might make me happy.

Sky was changing that.

Change was scary.

But, aside from all of that, they were right. I needed to talk to Beau. We needed to figure out what this was going to be. The last thing I wanted to do was hurt our friendship.

I didn't want to hurt him, but I also felt the need to hit that man upside the head. What the hell was he thinking? What was he gonna do? I needed to know what the fuck we were going to do.

How would he feel about me also being interested in Sky?

I let out a long groan and sat up, smoothing my hands over my hair.

It was about damn time we figured this out.

I wasn't going to go another day without understanding how Beau felt about me, and how he felt about this entire situation.

No more pretending.

It was time to rip the Band-Aid off.

I jumped up and snatched my hat, placing it and rolling my shoulders. I scowled as I stormed out of my room, straight across the house and past the kitchen, earning a couple curious glances from Boone and Winnie.

"Where the hell are you going all tensed up?" Winnie called.

"To deal with a *man*," I seethed.

The closer I got to his office, the angrier I got. Why in the hell had we been dancing around each other for so long? Was I not good enough for him? Was that it?

The office door was open. Beau was sitting at his desk staring at his computer like he was looking at a thousand ghosts. He looked up, his eyes widening as I stepped inside, shut the door behind me, and twisted the lock.

"We need to talk," I snapped.

I expected him to argue, but all he did was nod, blowing out a long breath. "I think we do as well."

At some point, he'd put on his mask. He mostly saved it for the rodeo, but occasionally would put it on around the ranch. I marched across the office and planted my palms on the desk, leaning forward to look him deep in his eyes. My heart skipped a beat the closer I got, every part of me craving him.

God, what was it about Beau? What was it about him that drove me so crazy?

"What are we doing?" I asked.

"We're talking."

I snorted. *Dammit.* "You know that's not what I mean. What are *we* doing?"

The corner of his mouth tugged. "You're gonna have to be more specific."

"Quit playing with me," I snapped. I closed my eyes for a second, searching for patience, and when I opened them, he was standing too.

He leaned in, his face just a couple of inches from mine.

"I am not good enough for you," he whispered. "I don't think I'm good enough for Sky. And yet I can't get either one of you out of my head. I've been dreaming about you for years, but I haven't done anything about it until now."

"Until now?"

He leaned forward, closing the distance between us. Shock rolled through me as his mouth pressed against mine, and I found myself tumbling into a kiss for the second time today.

This kiss was different. While the kiss with Sky was loaded with everything new and bright and beautiful, this kiss carried the weight of years of yearning. Years of dreaming that we'd one day cross this line, that we would find a way together. This was a kiss that I've been wanting since I was a teenager. It was a kiss with someone that knew me almost as well as I knew myself.

My fingers curled into the smooth linen of his button-down, and I yanked him forward. Our kiss deepened, a soft groan leaving me.

He cupped my face, letting out the softest whimper.

I loved a tough man who wasn't afraid to whimper.

As we drew back, we were breathless, and a fire was lit that would surely burn us all.

"I need more," I whispered.

"I want more," he answered. "Anything you want. *Anything*, Priscilla."

I searched his sweet brown eyes. My head was spinning.

We needed to think about this. We needed to think through *everything*. What about Sky? What about what would happen if we hooked up and it didn't work out? What then?

I drew back and turned away, planting my hands on my hips as I tried to reason with myself. This was the exact kind of situation I'd been trying to avoid, and yet here I was, going for it anyway.

Dammit. Damn it all to hell and back.

"Priscilla," he whispered. "Please look at me."

My god, I'd just kissed Beau. I'd kissed Sky! Was I losing it?

Why did it feel so damn right?

I heard him come around the desk behind me, his presence inching closer. His arms slid around me and he pulled me against him.

And he hugged me.

That was it. His arms were strong, his body a wall I could fully melt into. His touch wasn't sexual, wasn't flirtatious—it was just him. Holding me.

My eyes stung. It'd been a long time since I'd been held.

"I don't want to screw this up," I whispered.

"Me neither," he murmured. "It's scary. But I've never had a good thing happen to me in my life that wasn't."

I blinked back tears. He was right, though.

All the scariest decisions I'd made were the ones that worked out for the better. The decision to leave Oklahoma and go to college, getting a degree I wasn't sure was even right for me. Working my ass off to make enough money to build up savings. Meeting someone that ended up being toxic and then finding the will to actually leave him.

All of that had been scary.

But this?

This was a whole different level of scary. Butterflies erupted in my stomach, my chest squeezing as I let my nerves take over, giving into the panic for just a few seconds. All while he held me through it. Patient. Strong. Kind.

"Whatever you need from me," he murmured. "I don't care what it is, Pris. Whatever you need from me, you can have."

"I know," I whispered. "I just need you to keep doing this for a moment."

He let out a gentle hum, his arms tightening just enough to make me feel even safer. I closed my eyes, drew in a deep breath, and then let it out slowly. Counting to three.

And past the clouds of fear, there were rays of hope. Sparkling bright, shining right on the desires I'd held in my heart for so long that they were covered in dust and cobwebs.

"I don't want a casual relationship," I finally said. "I want to be loved. I want to be cared for. I want to love and care for the ones I'm with, too. And there's not a single sane soul in the world who learns that about me and stays."

"I'm not going anywhere."

"Then you've lost your mind."

Beau let out a soft snort. "Pris, I've been losing my mind about you for years."

My heart galloped in my chest. "I want Sky too."

"We both do," he said bluntly.

"So then we would be a trio . . ."

"Yes," he said. "We would be."

"And when they leave?"

"I don't want them to leave," he admitted softly. "But if they do, then we'll cross that bridge when it comes. And we'll still have each other."

Finally, I turned around in his arms, resting my palms on his chest and looking up at him. "Beau . . ." I whispered. "Are you sure? Everyone will know."

He swallowed hard. "I know. I want you, Pris. I've wanted you for years, but I just haven't pursued you because I didn't want to be that guy."

I blew out a breath, my head tilting as I studied him closely. "What *guy*? My boss?"

"Yeah," he said.

I scowled at him. "You're a good man, Beau Adams. A good boss, too, even though I give you a hard time about it. And while I understand why you never crossed this line before now, I wish you would have."

He pressed his forehead to mine, his eyes closing. "Me too."

"So . . . what are we going to do about it?"

He leaned back, his eyes sparkling with a hint of mischief. "What do you *want* to do about it? You already know I'd get on my knees for you."

My brows shot up. Sometimes, I felt like an open book around this man. "Oh would you, now?"

"I would." He straightened his spine, a smirk tugging. "Right now."

A few days of pure lust hit me like a freight train. "Beau . . ."

"I can take a break," he whispered, swallowing hard.

As crazy as it was, I wanted him to. "I'll meet you in your bedroom. Thirty minutes. Okay?"

He nodded slowly. "I'll be there."

I took a step back from him, and then another, until I felt the door knob behind me. "Are you sure?"

Beau smiled. "I'll see you in thirty minutes, Pris. In my room."

*Thirty minutes.*

Just enough time for me to wonder if I'd lost my damn mind.

# 10
# beau

THIRTY MINUTES FLEW BY FASTER than a tornado and slower than molasses. By the time I made it to my door, I wondered if I'd imagined everything. Kissing Sky, kissing Pris, us finally admitting that *something* had been between us for so long that we hadn't pursued.

I rapped my knuckles on the wood, glancing left and right for anyone else. It was still middle of the day, though, and the house was quiet. My pulse raced as my door swung open.

Pris' fingers curled into my button down and she yanked me forward with enough force that I stumbled in. The door shut behind us as she turned the lock, a heavy silence settling between us.

*Damn.* She was gorgeous. Everything about her was absolutely perfect. I had no idea why she would want anything to do with me, but I didn't have time to really second guess that.

She leaned up on her tiptoes, her soft, plush lips brushing mine. I groaned, my hands settling on her hips. In a swift motion, I lifted her so her legs could wrap around my waist. Her arms looped around my neck, heat bursting between us.

I couldn't get enough of her. After all of that yearning and pining, every touch was like holding a slice of heaven.

She drew back, catching her breath. "Fuck," she mumbled. "You're real good at that."

"So are you," I rasped.

"Put me down."

Reluctantly, I let her feet hit the floor. A bolt of surprise shocked me as she reached up and twined her fingers in my hair, giving me a gentle push.

"Kneel for me, cowboy."

My knees went weak and I slowly hit the wood floors, my head tipping back as Priscilla stepped closer to me, her gaze searching mine.

We'd been dancing around each other for years, but something about Sky showing up and drawing us together had shifted things. The tension in the air crackled with electricity, drowning the two of us like a flood.

Her expression softened, her hand sliding beneath my chin. As she pushed my face up, all of my attention was on her. On the way the sunlight glistened on her rich brown skin and haloed her curls. The way her beautiful dark brown eyes shone. More than anything else, I wanted to touch her. I wanted to worship her. I wanted to make up for all the years I'd dreamt about kissing her.

We'd been denying ourselves for far too long.

Priscilla's lips slowly curved into a smile, her fingers sliding around to the back of my head. "I'm taking off this mask, Beau. I want to see *you*."

Damned if I didn't whimper.

I couldn't say I was much of a smooth talker behind closed doors. I was a simple man, at the end of the day. And

I wished I could come up with all the flowery language in the world to really tell her how kneeling for her made me feel, but my voice faltered into a whisper.

"Can I touch you?" I asked as she pulled my mask free.

"Yes," she said. "I want you."

"I want you too. More than anything else."

"Then show me."

Lust whipped up like a storm, howling in my veins, as I reached for her, scooping her up and standing in one smooth motion. She stifled a squeal as I carried her to her bed, laying her down on the soft quilt. I grabbed her boot and tugged, slowly pulling it off. And then the other, putting them together on the floor. Her eyes sparkled with excitement as I kicked mine off and crawled onto the bed between her thighs, running my hands up the denim, cradling her body until my fingers met the top pearl snap of her button down.

Our lips met tentatively at first. Softly. The taste of her was heavenly, rocking me straight to my core. How many times had I imagined this moment?

Her body was hot against mine, heat pouring off us in waves as our kiss turned fiery. Her tongue swiped against mine, our groans blending together as she gripped my T-shirt and tugged it overhead. My heart skipped a beat as I planted a hand next to her head, staring down at her in wonder.

"I'm no good at words." I swallowed hard, cupping her cheek as I kissed her again. "But every single part of me is in awe of you, Pris."

Her breath hitched. I paused for a moment to admire her, but she shook her head, her hands running up my chest as if to urge me to get a move on.

"If we're away too long, someone will come looking for us," she said.

I snorted. "The door is locked. They can't stop us now."

There wasn't anything in hell or on earth that could pull me from her arms. Right now was about each other. Savoring every moment, every touch, satiating the deep longing that'd been haunting the two of us for far too long.

I popped the second button on her shirt. Pris hummed as I took my time, kissing down her neck and chest as I popped another. One by one, the soft snaps broke the silence through the bedroom.

Touching her just felt right. I grazed my knuckles over her collarbone and she sat up slightly, helping me pull her shirt free. I grabbed the hem of the tank she wore underneath and tore it away. All she wore now was her bra and jeans.

"Get these off," she demanded, tugging at my belt.

"So impatient," I teased.

But I rolled over quickly, unclasping my belt. She did the same, the two of us shucking off the rest of our clothes. They all landed in a pile on the floor and my eyes widened as she stretched out on my bed, now completely naked, her hands over her breasts.

All thoughts evaporated. My cock hardened as she slowly moved them, her dark brown nipples hard and begging to be sucked.

She was quicker than a Texas flood. In the blink of an eye, she was pushing me down and straddling my thigh, her fingertips grazing the jagged line that marred my hip. Her pussy was hot and wet against my skin, my cock throbbing in response.

"Where's that scar from?" she asked. "I've never seen it before."

"One of the horses kicked me years ago while I was shoeing them," I chuckled. "I fell down and one of the pritchels sliced me up. Learned a couple good lessons that day."

She shivered. "I bet that hurt."

"It did."

She hummed softly and leaned down, her lashing fluttering as she looked up at me. My lips parted in shock as she kissed the scar gently, and then traced the line with the tip of her tongue.

"Fuck," I rasped. "*Pris.*"

Her hand wrapped around the base of my cock, squeezing gently as she rocked her pussy against my thigh. My mind was short circuiting.

"I think we know who's the boss now," she said. "Right?"

The corner of my mouth tugged. "Do you wanna be the boss of me right now, darlin'?"

"If I don't, then we'll be here all day. All night." She rocked her hips as pre-cum beaded on the tip of my cock. I was all too aware of her bare pussy against my thigh. "We don't have time for that. I want you now."

"I want to savor you," I said.

"Tonight. Come to my bed tonight."

"I'm meeting Sky tonight . . ." I trailed off.

"Oh?" She smirked. "Really?"

My cheeks were burning. "Yes . . ."

"Maybe I'll join and watch. With both of your permission, of course."

That made me even harder. Before I could say another word, Pris leaned down and crushed my mouth with hers, her other leg throwing over my hip so that she was straddling me fully now. My cock slapped against her pussy, my fingers gripping each ass cheek as she grinded against me, her hands exploring my chest. Pleasure rolled through me as she pinched one of my nipples.

"Do you like that?" she asked.

"Yes," I huffed. "I like that a lot."

Shock followed as she replaced her fingertips with her lips, sucking gently. My eyes rolled back and it took every ounce of willpower to keep myself from groaning too loud. Sparks skated across my skin as she moved to the other, all while reaching down between us to stroke my cock.

I didn't know what to do with my hands. Hell, I couldn't remember the last time I'd been with someone, and I'd never been with someone who wanted to dominate me.

But I liked submitting to Pris.

There was something about it. Vulnerable, exciting. I could feel my thoughts vanishing, all tumbling down the path of submission. I just wanted to be good for her. I just wanted to please her.

My hips bucked, my hands tightening on her.

She smirked against me and then looked up. "That's my good boy."

*Good boy?!* My eyes widened as a rush of need overtook me. No one had ever called me a good boy before, and damned if it didn't confirm something I'd suspected about myself for a long time.

I had a praise kink.

"Where's the lube?" she asked.

"Now, wait a damn minute," I grunted. "You just called me a good boy."

She raised a brow. "Too much?"

"No—of course not," I stammered. "I . . ."

"Liked it?"

"Yes," I admitted.

Fuck. I really liked it. In fact, my mind was still spinning. No one had ever said something like that to me.

"I've been wanting to call you a good boy for years."

"Oh really?"

"Mm-hmm." Pris grinned. "Just seems like something you've needed to hear for a while."

"I think I agree, given how . . . how it made me feel."

"Good . . . Beau, *where* do you keep your lube?"

"Top drawer. Condoms, too. Although, they've probably gathered dust at this point."

Pris slid off me with a chuckle. "Well, time to dust them all off then, huh?"

I raised my head, my cock standing straight up as I watched her hips sway. She walked over to my dresser and pulled the top drawer open, pulling out a bottle of lube and a condom. My tongue was tied as she turned back to face me.

Gods, she was beautiful. I'd always thought so, of course. But seeing her like this, fully naked and aroused and walking straight toward me—I was the luckiest man alive. The luckiest damn man alive.

She knelt back onto the bed and I took the bottle from her, dragging her back on top of me. She laughed as she stretched out, the two of us kissing until we had to catch our breath.

"I want to ride you, cowboy," she said.

"Anything you want, darlin'," I huffed.

I felt around for the condom and opened it while she uncapped the bottle of lube. Between the two of us, we got it fit over my cock. She poured a generous amount into her palms and stroked me up and down, the liquid glistening. I pulled her to the side, her thighs part as I took the lube from her, pouring more onto my fingers and warming it before touching her. Dark curls gave way to her pussy, already shining from her wetness. My mouth watered as I studied her clit.

"I want to feast on you," I rasped. "I want to finger fuck you until you scream out my name."

"Beau," she gasped. "And you said you didn't have the words."

Maybe I did have them when it came to talking about what I wanted to do to her. "Tonight, when you come to me, we're going to take our sweet damn time. I don't care if I sleep a wink."

"Promise?" she teased.

I answered by pushing two fingers against her, spreading the lube over her pussy. She whined as I circled her clit slowly, fighting every instinct that screamed for me to bury my face between her thighs and spend the next hour eating her out and making her come on my face.

She arched as I carefully slid one finger inside her, and then a second, moving them in and out with ease. She was so wet, her pussy hot and needy. My cock felt the same way. I needed to be inside of her, needed to know what it was going to feel like to finally fuck her.

She planted her hand against my chest and shoved me back again, taking the reins.

Nerves suddenly fluttered like a thousand butterflies. "Are you sure?" I asked softly, swallowing hard.

"Yes. Are you?"

"Yes," I said, grabbing her hips and lifting her.

She squeaked as I sat her on top of me. A laugh bubbled up from her as she leaned forward, kissing me while I took hold of my cock and guided it to her entrance.

"I'll take it slow," she rasped softly.

Gently, she sat back, taking the first inch slowly. Pleasure popped like fireworks, my entire body humming in response as she carefully took more, her pussy clenching around me as she adjusted to my size.

"Fuck," she huffed.

"Too much? I can add more lube—"

"No," she hissed. "It's just been a long time and I'm taking it slow."

I nodded in understanding, hungrily watching her expression as she took more of me. She was so fucking wet and hot, her slick heat gripping me. I slid my hand down, resting my hand on her mound and pressing my thumb against her clit. Her head tipped back on a gasp, her hips circling as I did the same to her clit, following the same motions.

"Oh god," she moaned.

Pris worked my cock inside of her until she was fully seated, the two of us moaning together. My eyes fluttered as I didn't let up on her clit, maintaining the same languorous speed.

She felt so damn good. Her hands planted on my chest, her expression full of pleasure as she lifted and then sank back down. I moved my hips to meet her, a slow, drawn out rhythm falling into place between us.

Every movement was met with our bodies sliding against each other. I was fighting the urge to take over and fuck her harder, but I craved being good for her. I wanted her to use me however she wanted, to take my cock in whatever way pleased her most.

"Keep touching me there," she whimpered. "You feel so good."

"So do you," I huffed, working her clit.

I wasn't sure I was going to keep being able to form words. All I could do was focus on her taking my cock and me rubbing her clit, our bodies melting together. She leaned down, our lips locking as we fell into another heated kiss. She kissed down my jaw to my neck then the soft spot of my shoulder, biting down hard enough that I grunted, the pain flashing through me.

"Too much?"

"No," I rasped. "More. Please."

She bit me again, the pain going straight to my cock. I thrusted up in response as her teeth sank into my skin hard enough, I knew it'd bruise. And god, I wanted that. I wanted to wake up in the morning and see something she'd left on me, a mark of remembrance from our first time together. Something that would last for a few days.

"Fuck." I grabbed hold of her hips and thrusted up harder and faster as she peppered kisses and bites across my shoulders, occasionally offering me a kiss on the lips between whimpers and moans.

"I'm close," she gasped.

She sat up slightly, her hands on my pecs as her head fell back, her curls tumbling down her shoulders. She rocked her hips, taking me faster, meeting every stroke until we were heading straight to the edge.

Her body trembled, her hand slapping over her mouth as she yelped, her orgasms crashing into her. I took a few revered seconds to memorize every line of her face as she came, and then I lost control, my pleasure unleashing. Cum spurted from my cock in hot bursts as her body collapsed against mine.

She melted against me. Her head settled on my chest, rising and falling with each breath. The scent of sex filled the room. I closed my eyes, savoring her. Cherishing her.

Years. Ever since she'd come home to Rainbow Ranch, I'd pined for her.

Now, she was here in my arms.

Priscilla let out a soft laugh and raised her head, looking up at me. I grinned between heavy breaths, massaging her scalp gently. Her gaze glimmered with a sweetness that healed me.

"How was that?" I whispered.

She smirked. "Beau Adams, you know that was good."

I chuckled, pressing a kiss to her forehead. "It was perfect. I want more. . . kinky things . . ."

"Me too," she said. "We have a lot to explore, don't we?"

I nodded. "We do."

"A lot to explore with Sky too . . ."

My throat constricted. "Yes. We do. We should take every second we get with them."

"I agree. I hope you give them every ounce of pleasure you just gave me . . . and then I want to hear about it tomorrow."

I raised a brow, unable to stop a smile. "Yeah?"

"Yes." She stole another kiss. "Then I want to dance with them. And then with the two of you at the same time, if you know what I mean."

"I do."

"Good."

Pris winked and then slowly rolled off me right as a knock sounded at the door. We both jumped up, eyes wide.

"Beau! You in there?"

Dammit. *Of course*, it was Boone.

"Yeah! I'm busy!" I yelled.

"Have you seen Pris? I've been looking all over for her but she's nowhere to be found."

She pressed her lips together, looking over at me. I closed my eyes for a second and then shook my head. "Boone, she's in here with me."

"With *you*?"

"Can we get some privacy?" Pris said loudly.

"Well, I'll be." Boone's voice was full of shock and amusement. "I guess hell has frozen over."

"Boone," I warned.

"I'm gonna go bake a Better Than Sex Cake. Y'all got some explaining to do."

"Boone," we both exclaimed.

I heard his chuckle as his boots scuffed away. I shook my head again and then met Pris' gaze.

Then we both burst out laughing.

"Well," she said. "So much for secrets."

"I'd never keep being with you a secret, Pris."

# 11
# sky

WORD TRAVELED FAST on Rainbow Ranch about Beau and Pris. I felt a sense of satisfaction that I'd had a hand in bringing those two together. And while many people might feel jealous, all I felt was a sense of *excitement*.

I walked through the front door for dinner and wasn't surprised to see almost everyone already seated. The teens had gone home early today, so it was just the group of adults who ran the ranch tonight. My understanding was that there'd be a pride picnic this weekend since it was finally June, and I was thrilled to be here for it.

Winnie and Boone were putting food out on the table. Wylie, Billie, and Benny were all playing a lazy game of poker. Pris was leaning back in her chair with her arms crossed.

Beau was missing.

My heart lurched the moment she looked up at me. I could see her tense, but then I grinned, and she relaxed as I stole the chair next to her.

"Hey, cowgirl," I said.

Pris snorted and leaned forward, using her body to

block the two of us as she turned her head to look at me. "I was wondering where you've been."

"Oh, I got some work in," I said. "Used Beau's office while it was free, since no one else needed any help."

"Oh." Her cheeks warmed and she lowered her voice. "I feel . . ."

"Pris," I murmured, sliding my hand under the table. "I'm not jealous."

She let out a slow breath and then nodded. "Okay. I don't think we expected it."

"Will you two get a room?" Benny quipped playfully.

Pris sighed dramatically. "We'll return."

"Better make it quick," Boone called from the kitchen. "Beau should be here in five."

She stood up, taking my hand with her as she led me out of the dining room. I blushed as a few eyes followed us, but everyone seemed to be happy for whatever was developing. What that was, I wasn't entirely sure. But, it felt right.

And that's all that mattered, right?

Pris led me to a door frame between the living room and the hall, and backed me against it. I tipped my head back, my body anticipating her touch.

"Are you sure this is okay?" she asked.

I answered by leaning forward to kiss her hard. She froze for a second and then melted, her hands cupping my face. Pris pulled back and let out a deep hum.

"Does that answer your question?" I whispered.

"Sure does," she murmured.

"How are you and Beau?"

"Good. I don't think either one of us expected to fall into bed. It just happened, and then I worried about ruining this with you . . ."

"The tension has been brewing for a long time, it seems

like," I said. "And you didn't ruin anything. How many times should I say I like both of you? I like both of you, Pris. I like both of you a lot."

"Well . . . I know I like you. I know he likes you."

"Good," I teased. "Glad we got that established."

She wrinkled her nose. "Brat."

"I can brat if you want me to. Or I can get on my knees for you. Really, I'll do whatever you want . . ."

"Sky," she hissed.

The front door swung open and Beau stepped in, his gaze immediately lifting to us. As if pulled by an invisible force, he crossed the living room to us.

I swallowed hard as the tension was set to boiling. Pris reached up and grabbed his hat, and surprised us both by putting it on my head.

"Lovebirds!" Billie called from the dining room. "Get your butts to the table before Boone puts you in timeout!"

Pris snorted and then gave us a flirty wink. "The stars are out tonight. And Beau's got a truck. And no one will hear you when you moan. That's all I'm saying."

My mouth dropped as she sashayed away.

I started to take his hat off, but Beau shook his head. "Nope. I want you to wear my hat, little storm."

My mouth dropped *again*.

*Little storm.*

He dipped his head down and pecked my cheek, then gave me a little pull toward the dining room. I followed him in a daze to the dining room, blushing as I ended up in a chair between him and Pris.

"Let's eat," Boone said, clapping his hands together.

The initial awkwardness I felt soon melted as conversations flowed and food was passed around. It was a home-cooked meal of brisket, mashed potatoes, roasted carrots, collard greens, and fresh rolls.

"This looks amazing," I said. My mouth was watering. "I don't know how you cook like this all the time."

"He's amazing," Wylie said.

"Well, we gotta keep y'all fed for extracurricular activities," Boone teased.

Oh god. Everyone had a different reaction to that. I blushed so deeply, I felt like I was gonna melt out of my damn chair. Beau sighed and gave his twin brother a look. Pris snorted. Billie and Winnie barked out a laugh, Benny scrunched his face, Wylie shook his head.

"Pay him no mind," Beau sighed. "Anyway . . . How was everyone's day?"

"Just peachy," Billie said. "How was *yours*?"

He sighed again, but there was an ease between him and everyone that was comforting. They were giving him a hard time because they loved him, not because they had an issue with his choices.

"I need to get some sound-proofing material next time I'm in Johnson Springs," Benny said.

"Yep," Pris agreed. "I like that idea."

"I think we *all* like that idea," Billie said.

"Not to change the subject from my sex life, but we should talk about the picnic this weekend," Beau said.

"What about it?" Boone chimed. "We got all the food and things for it. About fifty people RSVP'd."

"*Fifty?*" I asked in disbelief. "All the way out here?"

"Oh, there'll be more," Pris said. "It's one of the only events like this in Oklahoma. We should have about two hundred people."

"That's amazing," I said. "Wow. You know, I've never been to a pride event."

"*What?*" everyone exclaimed together.

"Oh my god," Billie said excitedly. "We have a pride virgin in our midst."

"Careful, Billie," Boone said. "We don't want to scare them off."

"We do have to throw glitter on them," Benny said.

"Or, I can make a shirt that says *My First Time*," Billie teased.

"Billie," Beau sighed. "Really?"

"What? It's the truth! You can't deny us this."

I laughed, shaking my head at them as the four siblings went back and forth. My head spun as a realization hit me.

This felt like home.

More than any place had ever felt before.

Beau's hand settled on my right thigh under the table, and Pris' settled on my left. Being between the two of them with casual, comforting touches—my eyes stung with tears for a second before I managed to chase them away by biting into a soft roll.

Wylie cleared his throat. "They're going hog wild over this."

"They are," I said.

Winnie offered me a soft smile. "You get used to it the longer you're around."

"Do you?" Pris chuckled. "I've known them for years and always feel like I'm in a cowboy circus."

"Hey," Boone quipped. "You like cowboys."

"Damn right I do."

Everyone burst out laughing again, and the conversations settled into overlapping topics. The picnic, the horses, Noodles and Dennis' unlikely friendship, the strange lack of storms since I arrived on the ranch.

"Do you think we'll have more tornadoes?" Wylie asked me.

I nodded. "We're still in storm season for a bit. I'm sure a storm will brew up sometime soon."

"And will you go tornado hunting?" Winnie asked.

I nodded again. "Yep. That's the whole reason I'm out here right now. I've been keeping an eye on radar so when it does come up, I'll go chasing."

"Alone?" Boone asked.

"Yeah," I said. "It'll be okay. I used to have an assistant, but we had a falling out a few weeks ago. But when I first started, it was just me and the trusty van."

"What made you start storm chasing?" Billie asked curiously.

A slow breath left me. "Well, growing up, I lived in a small town that was torn apart by one. The community never truly recovered, honestly. It was a small, forgotten town that was leveled. We were lucky to have survived."

I could still remember the wind. Like a freight train barreling down on what little we owned, taking everything with it. Still to this day, I'd wake up from a nightmare of those moments as a child where I'd been certain I wouldn't see the sun again. I'd never forget my mom holding onto me, praying that we'd make it.

We did. We were lucky. There were many families in that town who didn't.

"I'm sorry," Beau murmured. "That sounds horrifying."

"It was," I said simply. "But that horrible situation made me wonder why we're not able to prevent the destruction. We have tornado sirens and warnings now, but we didn't get any sort of heads up when it happened. One minute I was playing in the yard, and the next, the sky was swirling green and it sounded like the world was being ripped apart. Since then, I've always wanted to help people. Whatever I can do to contribute to our understanding of how they work means I'm helping families, towns, and communities avoid unimaginable devastation."

Everyone nodded solemnly, and Pris gave my thigh a squeeze.

"I think it's amazing," she said. "And next time there's a storm, I'll go with you."

Beau gave my thigh a squeeze. "Me too."

I raised a brow. "I guess I have room for two."

"Good," Pris said, letting out a soft laugh.

She'd been right about Beau, of course. That he'd want to join us if the chance arose.

"It can be dangerous though, right?" Boone asked.

"It can be," I admitted. "I have a good sense, though."

There'd been a lot of close calls over the years, but somehow I'd always managed to escape. It was as if my instincts took over and I was able to pull out of the way, or into a spot that the worst of the tornado would miss.

"Besides, I'm really just there to take pictures and to gather data. Then I send all that information to a group of scientists, and they take it from there. Can't say it pays a lot, but it's work I feel good about."

"You should live here," Benny said lightly. "You'll see all the storms in Oklahoma, and then when it's not the season for it, you could work with Pris."

My eyes widened. I opened my mouth to say that I'd like that, but Pris cleared her throat. "I'm sure they'll be ready to be done with us by then."

That wasn't true. I looked over at her as a moment of awkwardness passed, but Boone filled it quickly.

"Well, I've got some chocolate cake for everyone," he announced. "Someone help me bring all the things out."

"I'll help," Wylie said, jumping up before anyone else could.

I leaned back in my chair as everyone started to chat amongst themselves again. I looked over at Pris again, but she wouldn't look at me.

What if I stayed? What would happen then?

Usually in the storm off-seasons, I picked up a job wherever I could. Would work for a few months then move on.

But I was ready to put down roots.

I was ready to stop only chasing my dreams. I wanted something more.

I deserved something more.

But was that *more* here? At Rainbow Ranch?

With Pris and Beau?

A shimmering ray of hope broke through my thoughts. *Maybe.* Just maybe, it was.

# 12
# beau

AFTER A NOSY DINNER with our ranch family, I was ready to escape with Sky. We stepped out into the cool night, the front door slowly swinging shut. They went to the railing and leaned over it, looking up at the stars.

"We don't have to go stargazing if you don't want to," I said. "But I do have the truck, and it's beautiful out here."

"I'd love to," they said. "Do we need anything?"

"No, I already packed everything," I said softly.

Sky turned to face me, their cheeks dimpling as they offered a shy smile. "So you already packed everything, but still gave me the opportunity to back out of it?"

I took a step closer. "I like being prepared," I murmured. "And I wouldn't want you to do anything you aren't comfortable with. Ever."

"Well, I want to go stargazing with you, Beau. Really."

I smiled and offered them my hand. They slid theirs into mine, their palms smooth against my calluses. "Let's go."

"What about Pris?" they asked.

"Well, the agreement we came to is that we'll spend

time tonight together. Then maybe at some point the two of you can. And then maybe the three of us can . . ."

Their breath hitched as I led them down the porch steps to the gravel, leading them to the garage where my truck waited, all packed up.

"I like that," they said, and then let out a soft chuckle. "Not one bed, but one truck, huh?"

I grinned. "Well, truthfully, I think this truck has seen the most action out of any of us. It's just good to drive out. And nothing beats a clear spring night in Oklahoma."

"I believe it," they said.

My truck was my pride and joy, and far too big for its own good. I opened up the door for Sky, and before they could start climbing up, I lifted them into the front seat.

"Whoa," they laughed, their hand curling into my shirt and tugging me forward.

Our lips met in a heated kiss. I melted against them on a soft moan.

"I've been thinking about you all day," I whispered.

"I've been thinking about you, too," they said.

The three of us were moving fast. Maybe a little too fast for a lot of people, but it felt right. And I was going to claim every moment I could with Sky, especially if they were going to leave.

Sky pressed their forehead against mine, and then gave me a gentle pat on the chest.

"We better get going," I mumbled.

"Yeah," they whispered. "We have stars to look at, huh?"

I chuckled and shut the door, going around to the driver side. I got in and cranked on the engine, the truck roaring to life. I glanced back at the house as I drove down the road that stretched across the entire ranch.

An easy silence settled between the two of us, and I knew we were both lost in our thoughts.

I wondered what they were thinking about, though.

Headlights beamed, casting light over the gravel road and fields.

"How did you end up running a ranch?" Sky asked softly.

I cleared my throat, thinking about where to start. "Well, the four of us have lived here our entire lives. I always knew I was going to end up running it, and always wanted to. It always felt right for me, you know?" I breathed out slowly, my hands tightening on the steering wheel. "Our parents passed away in a wreck about seven years ago, leaving the four of us. It was hard. We were broken. But we still had each other, and I know they'd be proud of what we've done with the place since then."

"I know they would be, too," Sky said. "It's something special, Beau. It really is."

I glanced over at them and smiled, then veered off the road into the grass toward the middle of the field. There was a spot that was slightly elevated and would give us the best views, along with the privacy we wanted.

Sky rolled down the window and leaned their head out as I slowed looking up at the stars. They let out a breathless sigh. "It's gorgeous."

"Just you wait," I said.

I stopped the truck in a spot where the grass was already smoothed down. It was *the* spot to stargaze and over the years, the earth had trained itself to the dent of our tires. My boots hit the ground as I hopped out and opened the back door.

A couple quilts, a couple pillows, and a packed bag full of other necessities in case we ended up having sex. And while I wasn't a fool—I knew we'd probably end up exploring each other's bodies—that wasn't the entire goal here.

I wanted to treasure every sweet moment with them I could.

Although sex would be good, too . . . Between Sky and Priscilla, something had awakened deep inside me, and my thirst was unquenchable. I had a feeling the only thing that would satiate me was being with them together, at the same time.

Because how could I not want either one of them? Sky and Priscilla were both perfect. My thoughts have been filled with them every waking moment over the last week.

I had a feeling that after tonight, I'd never go another moment without them on my mind.

Sky jumped out of the truck. "Need help with anything?"

"Nope," I said. "I'll get it set up."

I tossed everything into the bed of the truck and climbed up with practiced ease, kicking my boots off and setting them on the ledge. The truck bobbed as I spread out the blankets, moving back and forth as I made us a little bed. Sky watched with a sweet smile, resting their forearms on the ledge next to my boots.

"You're cute when you're flustered," they said dreamily.

I laughed, shooting them a hungry look. "Who's submissive here?"

They grinned. "Oh, definitely me. Doesn't mean I can't tease you, though."

"True." I finally had the blankets and everything set up the way I wanted. I reached down and grabbed the latch to the tailgate, patting the metal. "Come on up."

Sky went around to the gate and I held out my hand, helping them up. They kicked off their shoes and crawled in, settling down on the blankets and sitting cross legged.

Their head tipped back as they looked up at the stars, their expression bringing me pure joy.

"Wow," they whispered. "This is amazing, Beau."

My heart thundered in my chest. There was just something about them. Their kindness. Their strength. Their bravery. I wanted to spend all my time getting to know them.

Sky grinned as I settled down next to them, and reached out to cup my face.

I drew them in for a kiss. It was sweet at first, gentle and timid. They let out a soft hum, their tongue swiping over mine before they released a heavy sigh.

"You okay?" I checked in.

"Oh yes. Just never thought there'd be a day where I ended up in the back of a truck with a cowboy while stargazing."

I chuckled, leaning back and stretching out. I put the bag to the side, and they raised a brow, nodding their head toward it.

"What's in there?"

"Well . . . I brought some items in case we have sex. But just in case. There's no pressure, of course."

"*Oh.*" Their head tossed back on a laugh. "Beau, you know how bad I want you, right? We don't need to dance around wanting each other."

*Oh.* Good thing it was dark outside, because they probably couldn't see me blush so hard I was certain my face was the color of a ripe tomato. I laid my hands beneath my head, turning my attention to the vast skies above us. They settled down next to me, their head resting on my arm as they looked up.

"Amazing," they whispered. "I love it out here."

I smiled as I took in the views. It'd been a long time since I'd taken a few moments to appreciate the world around me in this way. The galaxies above us swirled in a vast sparkling tapestry, reminding me of how small we were in the universe.

And how damn lucky I was.

This far out, we didn't have the light pollution many cities and towns had. We didn't have anything obscuring the view. It was just land and night and humans and animals and everything between.

It was just me and Sky.

"I see the Big Dipper," they murmured.

"Show me."

They pointed, guiding my gaze to the cluster.

"So it is," I said, spotting the famous ladle.

"And then there's Canes Venatici, right under the Big Dipper handle . . ." They moved their hand, pointing out another group.

"You know a lot about stars."

"I know a lot about useless things," they chuckled. "But I don't know. Maybe it's in my name, but I've always liked looking up."

I reached up, slowly curling my hand around theirs. "I don't think anything you know is useless."

Their fingers intertwined with mine. I brought them down to my lips, gently pressing a kiss on top of their knuckles and noting there were a couple scratches.

"What happened here?" I asked curiously.

"Oh, it's from working in the garden," they said. They rolled over, resting their arms and head on my chest as they looked at me. "Maybe I'll eventually have rough hands like you, cowboy."

I smirked. "Maybe. If you stick around, you sure will."

Their grin softened. "We'll see. I like the idea of it. It's hard to want to leave when everything feels so nice here."

"You're always welcome," I whispered. "Always."

"Thank you. I want to know . . . about your kinks. Or whatever you're into. What you want."

"Well," I blew out a long breath. "I should make a laundry list of them, huh?"

They chuckled. "Not a bad idea."

"I'm a switch," I said. "Although I don't think I've ever submitted to a partner until, well . . ."

I cleared my throat, but Sky snickered. "Until Pris? Lucky man."

"I do feel lucky." Once again, my cheeks were hotter than two cast iron skillets. "Um . . . but, well, I love giving and receiving praise. Can't say I like degradation. But I *love* submission. I love playing with rope, too."

"All that knowledge of lassos . . ."

"Yup. Comes in handy."

"I bet Pris would have you tie me up and take me."

*Damn.* I let out a low growl. "I bet she would . . . I also enjoy spanking, gags, maybe even some wax play. I have a few candles that are safe for the skin that would be fun to play with."

"I love wax play," they breathed out. "It puts me into such a submissive headspace. It's like I'm floating in the clouds."

I nodded. "I'd like to try that. What about you, Sky? What do you like?"

"Well I like everything you mentioned, except I'm not a switch. I'm submissive all the way. I love giving pleasure and serving. I love doing what I'm told and being taken care of, in a way. When I'm pleasing my partner, I feel the best. It just satisfies something deep inside me."

"Mmm. I like that."

They smirked. "I also like being spanked. I like a little pain. Makes the pleasure all the more sweet. I love the idea of you holding me down while Pris does whatever she wants to me. Or even being tied up and used."

Fuck. My cock stirred, begging me for more. "I've had the same fantasy this week," I whispered.

"Oh really?"

Their sweet eyes widened slightly and then they leaned forward, kissing me.

"Seems like a match made in heaven," they said.

"I agree."

This time, my hands slid down to their waist and I threaded my fingers through their belt loops, pulling them fully on top of me. They straddled my hips, my cock stirring as they rocked them.

I dragged them down into another kiss. God, I needed them. I needed to feel them, be with them. I needed to prove just how much I'd been wanting them since they came tumbling into our life.

Sky leaned back. They were wearing a white button-down tucked into washed Levi's, their belt buckle gleaming as they unclasped it. I grabbed their hands and shook my head.

"Let me," I said. "I want to undress you."

"I want to do whatever you want me to."

I swallowed hard and sat up with their legs wrapping around me, fully seated against my body. I trailed kisses down the side of their neck, enjoying their soft moan as I gripped their hair.

"Fuck," they rasped. "I like that. I like submitting."

My cock throbbed against my zipper. "I know," I rasped. "Tell me if I do too much. Please."

"I'll say yellow if I need you to slow down or red if I need you to stop."

"Good," I praised. "You're the perfect little storm."

Sky whimpered as I grabbed hold of their belt and tugged it free, tossing it to the side. Their hands rested on my shoulders, squeezing my muscles as I unbuttoned their jeans and untucked their shirt. My fingers moved fast, undoing each button until I could pull their shirt free, revealing a sports bra underneath that compressed their breasts.

"Fuck," I groaned. "You're stunning, Sky."

They swallowed hard as I pushed them back into the blankets, hovering above them as I helped pull the rest of their clothes free. Within a few seconds, they sprawled out naked beneath me, aside from the black boxers they wore.

Their nipples hardened as a cool breeze caressed us. I caught one between my lips, sucking gently as they ground their hips.

"Oh god," they moaned. "*Yes.*"

The pretty sounds they made sent bolts of pleasure through me. Sky tugged at my shirt and I leaned back, stripping quickly despite intending to take my time with them.

Sky's eyes widened as they looked at the outline of my cock in my boxers. "Damn," they whispered. "We're gonna have to take this slow."

"We will," I promised. "I'm not going anywhere fast, darlin'. We've got all night if we want."

They quirked a brow. "Don't you have a ranch to run? Sleep seems important . . ."

"Being with you is more important," I said. "I'll get

plenty of sleep after making you scream loud enough that the stars remember your name."

Their mouth dropped as I lowered myself between their thighs, pushing them apart. Pulling their boxers free, I was finally rewarded with the beautiful sight of them completely naked beneath the starlight.

I settled down between their legs, holding their gaze as I pressed a gentle kiss to their pussy. Sky bucked their hips, a gasp following.

I pushed their thighs back, rolling my tongue against their clit. The sound of their voice grew louder as I slid two fingers against their entrance, feeling how damn wet they were.

Completely soaked.

"Oh my god," they groaned. I felt their fingers curl into my hair, giving me a light shove.

I lifted my head, raising a brow. "What's wrong? Am I going too fast?"

"No," they whimpered. "I just didn't realize how wet I was."

"You are wet," I said, licking my lips. "I can't wait to lick it all up. You're not embarrassed about it, are you?"

"A little," they admitted.

I shook my head. "This is hot as fuck, Sky."

"I've been told I get too wet before, which I know is a silly problem since a lot of people have the opposite issue, but—"

"Nothing about this is silly or a problem," I said. "And everything about you is perfect. Now, turn off that pretty head of yours and look up at the skies while I make you come."

"Fuck," they mumbled, plopping back down into the blankets.

Time to try this again. This time, I clamped my hand down over their hips, applying the type of pressure that would keep them from squirming too much. Then I lowered my face between their thighs, pressing it against their pussy. I dragged my tongue over their clit, circling it as soft moans floated on the breeze.

I dipped two fingers inside them with ease, working slowly. I wanted them to be drenched by the time I fucked them.

All the things I've been dreaming about doing to them came roaring back. Over the last few days, I'd had so many different fantasies. I'd lost track. One of them was this. Having them splayed out before me, allowing me to feast and pleasure them.

Whether I was in a top space or a bottom space, one thing was consistent—I loved bringing my partner pleasure. Doing whatever I could to make them come was the only thing on my mind.

They took two of my fingers deeper, my tongue still working their clit. I found a good rhythm, one that had them rising. They were strong, too, bucking against my hand that was splayed out over them. I clamped my forearm over them, holding them in place.

"Yes," they gasped. "Fuck. Fuck, that feels so good, Beau. Please don't stop."

I kept up the pace, listening to all the gorgeous sounds they made. The moans and cries growing louder as they abandoned any sort of reservation.

This was what I'd been craving. *Needing.*

I added a third finger, feeling a wave of shock as they took it. Their fingers curled into my hair, gripping and holding me in place. I continued to circle their clit, their thighs clamping around my head as I fucked them with my mouth and hand.

Their voice grew louder, more desperate. Their muscles coiled, their entire body winding up as they got closer and closer to the edge.

I wasn't going to stop until they came, not for a single second.

A deep wave of satisfaction rolled through me. I was finally getting a taste of Sky.

*Damn, I'm lucky.* That was all I could think as I was rewarded by the taste of them.

Their voice rang out and back arched as their orgasm crashed into them, their body tense as they came. I kept thrusting my fingers in and out as they rode it, and then gasped as hot liquid gushed from them.

"Oh my god," they cried

I didn't let them roll away, didn't let up even as they squirted on me. I lapped up the mess, reveling in the fact that I'd made them come so damn hard they squirted.

"I'm sorry," they gasped.

"What on earth are you sorry for?" I growled.

I rose up, my cock standing so hard that it was almost painful. How could I convince them that was the most beautiful thing I've ever seen? That I would be remembering this moment for as long as I lived?

They panted, lips parting in surprise as I brought the fingers that just been inside them to their mouth.

"Open up," I demanded.

They did as I asked, sucking themselves off me. Their tongue swirled around my fingers, all while they melted into the blankets. We'd made a mess, but I wasn't done yet, and of course, the blankets were waterproof anyway. So it didn't matter how messy we got.

I always thought things through.

"I need you inside me," they whispered.

And I needed to be inside them. I leaned back, freeing myself of the last piece of clothing. My cock sprang free, hard and throbbing. I've been hard for so long, just touching myself nearly sent me over the edge. But I'd been alive long enough to know that I could control the urge.

But it took every ounce of strength in order to do so.

I leaned back and grabbed the bag I brought with me. I reached inside, pulling out a condom and opening it quickly. Sky reached down between their legs, circling their clit with their fingers as they watched me put it on.

I made a mess," they whimpered.

"We're gonna make an even bigger mess, little storm."

I moved between their thighs, planting a hand above their head as I pressed the head of my cock against them. They tilted their hips back, and we both groaned together as they took me.

Sliding into them felt like sliding into heaven, their pussy milking me as they slowly took every inch. I made sure they had time to adjust me before they took me to the hilt, and then we both went still for a moment, savoring each other's bodies.

"Fuck," they moaned. "You feel so good. I can feel you stretching me."

All I could do was grunt.

My eyes fluttered as I waited patiently, waiting until they finally moved their hips, giving me the signal to move as well. I drew back slowly, and then pumped forward, filling them again.

Their hands settled on my shoulders, their nails biting into my back as we set a slow rhythm. In and out, our bodies merging together in the cool Oklahoma night.

I thrusted, peppering kisses on them between moans. After a few thrusts, the rhythm became more fevered, as if something wild was unleashed. Hot pleasure rushed through my body as I fucked them harder, the truck rocking back-and-forth as I took them. Their arms wound around my shoulders and neck, their legs around my waist. Every single movement had us both groaning and crying, our voices blending together.

We had so much to learn about each other. So much time to claim together. But all I could think about right now was how lucky I was to not only have kissed them, but to be with them, too.

To be with them, to be with Pris.

"I'm so close again," they rasped.

"I am too," I grunted.

"I want you to come. Please, please, please. Come inside me."

*Fuck*. Their hand slid between us and they rubbed their clit as I fucked them faster, driving in and out mercilessly. I just couldn't get enough of them.

They arched against me with a cry, another climax taking hold. The moment they clenched around me, I couldn't resist any longer. I gave one final thrust and moaned as I came hard, pleasure bursting through me.

The two of us melted against each other, the only sounds now coming from our breaths and the thunder in the distance.

*Thunder?*

I raised my head slightly, and so did Sky. Far off, we could see the occasional lightning strike dancing through clouds—but it was still clear above us.

"Beautiful," they murmured.

I had to agree.
They were.

# 13
# priscilla

Raindrops glistened under the early morning sun, the sky bright pink with a band of gray in the distance from the storm that'd passed over us.

The air was crisp, the garden ready to be worked. I pulled my gloves on and rolled my shoulders, thinking about all I needed to get done.

Also, very specifically, thinking about Beau and Sky.

I knew they'd come home in the middle of the night because I'd heard his boots on the wood floors and the soft click of Sky's door. I wondered how their evening had gone, and couldn't help but glance at the house occasionally, searching for Sky.

The heart moved faster than the head at times, I knew that much to be true. I'd spent the morning wondering how in the hell I was falling so damn fast—for someone I'd known for years and someone I'd only known for days.

I was cautious, reasonable. And yet, those two had my heart and mind's wires crossed.

"Morning."

I startled, my muscles tensing and then relaxing as I

turned to see Beau at the garden gate. He leaned over the fence as I walked up to him.

"Look who it is," I said, smirking as I approached.

He looked more tired than usual, and yet his eyes were brighter than the rising sun. I stopped right in front of him and he reached down, tipping my chin up and planting a kiss on my lips right in front of god and everybody.

"How was your night?" I asked softly.

"Wonderful," he murmured, kissing me again. "We thought about you."

My head spun as he offered a sweet smile. "Thought about me?"

"Mm-hmm. Several times."

"I see." I arched a brow. "Dare I ask what the context was?"

"You already know," he chuckled.

"I bet it was the same way we thought about Sky when we were together."

He nodded. "It was."

My cheeks warmed. "What am I gonna do with the two of you, Beau Adams?"

"Share a bed with us? Maybe even a life?"

I laughed, and reached up, squeezing his bicep. "Weird way to propose, but sure."

His cheeks reddened as I winked and spun, heading back to the patch of vegetables I was harvesting.

"I'll see you at lunch," I said over my shoulder.

"You sure will," he called.

I snorted as I squatted down by the green bell peppers and reached for the shears.

Mornings like this were my favorites. It wasn't too hot out, we'd have fresh produce for the Y'all Pride Picnic this weekend, and I got to do what I loved. I got lost in my work, forgetting all my worries and concerns until I heard the squeak of the gate.

I expected to see Beau, but Sky walked toward me wearing a denim shirt and loose jeans, a dimpled grin on their face.

"Well, well, well," I teased. "Someone is up late."

"Late?" Sky laughed. "All of y'all get up too early."

They kissed the top of my head before kneeling down next to me, looking around at the patch.

"I want to tell you everything," they said. "But don't want to overstep—"

"I think we're past that," I snorted. "I want to hear everything."

Sky breathed out, planting their hands on their thighs. "He calls me little storm."

My brows shot up—because damn, that man. That was the perfect nickname for Sky. "I love that."

"Me too . . . And stargazing was a great idea . . ."

"Did you actually see any stars or were you seeing *stars*?"

Sky's laugh rang through the garden. "Both. I got both."

"Good." I smirked and bumped their shoulder with mine playfully. "So. Tell me more."

"That cowboy is hot."

"He definitely is," I agreed. "And one lucky son of a gun. Two in one day."

Sky laughed again and then surprised me by leaning over, resting her cheek on my shoulder. "I really like you, Pris."

"I really like you too," I whispered, swallowing hard. "I feel like I'm a mess, though."

"Aren't we all?"

Well, we were. But . . .

"What would happen if I stayed?" they whispered.

I stiffened. "Is that really what you'd want? To live out here on a rural ranch with no cell service?"

"It feels right," they said. "It feels like home."

"You're just feeling that because of me and Beau."

They shook their head. "It's more than just the two of you. For the first time in my life, I feel like I belong somewhere. And I don't mind the hard work. I think it'd be good for me when I'm not storm chasing. Plus, when it is storm season, I'd be at the center of it all. It makes sense, doesn't it?"

"Making sense and it being right for you can be two different things." I breathed out slowly, trying not to get my hopes up. "I want you to stay, of course. But I never want someone to make a life-changing decision because of me. Or because they feel like they have to."

Sky was quiet for a moment. "Did you have something like that happen to you?"

My chest squeezed. "Yes," I admitted.

I didn't talk about it very often, but there were days where that part of my life felt like a nightmare that would never go away. I hated that someone had made me feel like less, when I knew I was worthy of everything good.

Beau knew some of the story. Not all, but some.

Now it was time for me to tell Sky.

"I was married once. For a couple years, to a man named Jacob. And we were really good together at first, but it went downhill fast. I wasn't allowed to be in control of my life or really anything. It took a lot of courage to finally leave him."

"You're courageous," they said. "And strong. One of the strongest people I've ever met."

I blinked back tears. "Sometimes I just want to be soft though, you know?"

Sky nodded gently. "I do. You can be soft with me. And Beau."

I snorted, fighting the tears until I really couldn't. "I'm scared of falling in love and losing myself."

"When you fall in love with the right person, they'd be there to remind you of who you are. If you got lost, they'd help lead you back. They'd be there to support you and love you and cherish you." Sky swallowed hard, looking up at me. Sunlight highlighted the side of their face, turning their irises to honey. "Call me a hopeless romantic, Pris, but that's what I feel when I think of you and Beau."

I sniffled and they reached up, gently thumbing away a tear.

It was scary to feel all of these emotions. It made me feel like I was falling.

But maybe I was falling into something good.

Maybe I was falling right where I needed to land.

# 14
# sky

Sᴡᴇᴀᴛ ᴅʀᴇɴᴄʜᴇᴅ my shirt as I stood up, twisting side to side to stretch my back. I was gonna be so sore, I could already feel every muscle protesting.

Although *maybe* that was from the activities in the truck last night.

My cheeks reddened at the thought of Beau. I'd never forget last night as long as I lived.

Being sore was worth it—whether it was from gardening or . . . *plowing*? Getting plowed?

There was something deeply satisfying about working in the garden, though. I could see why Pris loved it. Working with the earth, harvesting things that we would actually eat, and knowing that Boone would turn them into something delicious. It made it all the more fun to be here, even though I felt gross right now.

"Here," Priscilla said.

I looked up as she handed me a water bottle, and took it eagerly. The water was cool against my lips as I took a long sip, quenching my thirst.

But there was something else entirely that I was still thirsty for.

We'd kissed a couple of times now.

I'd been with Beau.

The two of them had been together.

But what about the two of us?

What about the *three* of us?

Was I moving too fast? *Maybe.* My entire life, I'd always had a tendency to just jump right in. Sometimes you had to trust that wherever you landed, you would be okay.

For the most part, it worked out. Sure, I got some bruises along the way, but the path led me here—right?

My heart said yes to staying at Rainbow Ranch. I was going to take some more time to think about it, but I could always leave if I wanted to . . .

I wasn't trapped here, even if I decided to stay.

And knowing that I had the freedom to leave whenever I wanted reminded me even more about why I could stay.

Everything I told the two of them was true. I did enjoy working on the ranch, at least what I'd done so far. I loved the horses and going to the stables. I especially loved Dennis. Even some of the teenagers I'd met were fun. I could see why they loved coming here—I would've loved it too when I was their age.

This place was magic. Something about the landscape kissing the crisp blue skies. Something about the acceptance and love that was so clear to see. Everyone was like a giant family, and while I knew that not everything was sunshine and rainbows, it still felt like it.

It felt good knowing that people had each other's backs —that they had someone to rely on. That type of family was rare, and it wasn't even about blood.

Family by the bonds of trust—the kinds of relationships that lasted forever.

It was something that I'd been missing for a long time.

*Community.*

When I came out as non-binary, I lost most of my family. A couple of cousins kept in touch on social media, but for the most part, I was on my own. Since college, I'd been fighting my way through life, running after whatever made me happy with everything I had.

Giving it all my best.

Life was too damn short to only go halfway.

Just like life was too damn short to give up on the chance to fall in love with two amazing people.

Pris let out a long moan. "I need a cold shower."

"Me too," I said.

I slowly looked up at her, and she raised a brow. There was silence for one beat, then two, then—"I have a theory that we could both fit in the shower."

"I think we should test that theory," I said, taking a step closer to her.

"I think we should . . ."

Pris glanced around the garden then pulled off her gloves, signaling that we were officially done with work for the day. Never mind that it was a couple hours early. Between the two of us, we'd gotten a lot done, so I wasn't worried if she wasn't.

Besides, I definitely needed a cold shower with a hot woman, no matter the time of day.

My eyes drifted over Pris as I followed her back to the house. We slipped inside without drawing any attention, which was a damn miracle in this house.

The moment we hit the hallway, Pris turned and grabbed me by the shirt, pulling me into a kiss. I wound my arms around her neck as she backed me against the wall, the two of us groaning together. We backed up into her room and she broke away with a gasp.

"We need towels and clothes to change into," she said quickly.

"I'll grab my stuff," I said.

We were on a damn mission. I rushed to my room and grabbed my towel, a T-shirt, and loose sweats, meeting her in the hallway. We both stared for a second, and then she grinned, the two of us bursting into laughter.

"We're a mess," she said.

"We're about to be even messier."

"*Sky.*"

I smirked as I followed her down the hall to the bathroom. The moment the door was locked behind us, we set our things down on the vanity and she pinned me against the wall.

I'd never get tired of kissing her. I whimpered as her teeth tugged my bottom lip, our tongues swiping against each other. Her fingers worked the buttons of my shirt until cool air rushed against my bare skin. Our clothes drifted to a pile on the floor piece by piece, until we were both naked.

My eyes widened as I took her in. She was stunning. I reached up and slid my hand behind her neck, kissing down her neck, down her chest to her breasts. Her nipples hardened as I cupped and teased them, enjoying the sound she made.

"Sky," she moaned. "I've been wanting this since the moment I saw you."

"Me too," I rasped.

Her fingers gripped the back of my head and I grunted as she turned my gaze up to hers. Just the tug on my hair sent a shiver down my spine, already edging me toward a submissive headspace.

"I want to please you," I whimpered.

"I know you do," she said.

My knees slowly sank to the floor and I knelt in front of her, feeling a sense of awe rush over me as it hit me how much I already cared for her. Somehow, I'd found two people in the world that were perfect for me.

"Mm," she hummed. "I like to see you on your knees."

"I love being here."

Her fingertips raked through my hair and I moaned, my eyes shutting as she teased me. I ran my hands up her calves, her skin soft against mine.

She took a step back and flipped on the shower. I stayed put as she grabbed her shower cap and pulled it over her curls, tucking any strays away. My eyes widened as she stepped beneath the shower head and then crooked a finger.

"Come on," she said. "Let's *cool* off."

I could be in an ice bath, and I'd still be anything but cool. I joined her in the stall and gasped as the water hit me, the momentary shock of cold drowned by the heat of her body pressing against mine.

"Fuck," she moaned.

Our hands roamed over each other, the chill of the water spreading goosebumps across my skin. My nipples hardened, a groan leaving me as she kissed down my neck and sucked one of them gently, teasing me until I was completely undone.

"I want to please you," I whimpered.

She drew back and reached for the body wash. "We're going to wash off and go back to my room, and I promise you'll get all the pleasing in you desire."

I wrinkled my nose at her, which made her laugh. She shoved the bottle into my hands and raised a brow, swapping spots with me so I was under the water.

"Get to washing me," she said.

*Oh.* Of course. I swallowed hard as I poured a dime sized amount into my palms and put the wash back on the shelf. I paused to turn the water just a little warmer, making it tepid as I lathered up the soap and reached for her. She let out a long moan as I ran my hands down her body, bubbles sliding over her nipples as I took my time to massage her breasts, and then moving them down her waist to her hips. I took my time to cherish every part of her until she grabbed my wrist, and spun us again.

Water rinsed down my back, and she poured more soap in her hands, returning the favor. My head fell back as she touched me, my breath hitching.

"Fuck," I moaned. "That feels good. Too good."

"There's no such thing as too good," she said, tugging me close.

The shower rinsed the soap off our bodies, leaving us wet and in need of more. She flipped off the shower and we got out. She tugged her shower cap free and put it away, the two of us drying off quickly.

"Do you think we can sneak down the hall in our towels?" I asked.

She tightened hers around her and then cracked the door, peeking out. "Hmm. Maybe. Let's go."

"Fuck," I laughed, scooping up my clothes as the door swung open and Pris ran down the hallway.

I followed after her, the two of us tumbling into her bedroom and slamming the door shut in a cloud of giggles. She flipped the lock and then turned to face me with a grin, letting her towel drop.

"God," I groaned. "You're gorgeous, Pris."

She smiled softly and then pointed to the bed. "Go wait there for me."

"Yes, ma'am," I said, dropping my towel and clothes.

I went to her bed and crawled onto the mattress, turning to watch as she went to her closet and opened the door. I was curious as to what she was pulling out, and my mouth dropped as she drew out what I knew to be a sex saddle.

"Oh my god," I said. "Those things are pricey."

"They are. Damn worth the money, though. Everything is clean and maintained, and the toy I'll attach is new and unused. But if you have a toy of your own you'd rather try, we can attach it . . ."

My cheeks warmed as I watched her spread a water-proof blanket out on the floor before placing the mound on top.

"Did Beau tell you I squirt?" I mumbled.

Pris brows shot up and she smirked. "He did not. Oh, I can't wait to watch your face while that happens. That's hot, Sky."

*Oh god.* Now my cheeks were flaming as she set every-thing up.

"Did you want to grab your own?"

I shook my head. "I didn't bring any with me . . ."

"Oh boy. No toys?!"

"I mean, there are other ways . . ."

Pris sat the dildo on top. It was about five inches long and in shades of pink, orange, and white.

Pris planted her hands on her hips and then turned to face me. "You know, I didn't even ask if you wanted to try this. Do you want to?"

"I definitely do," I said enthusiastically. "I want to do everything with you."

She smiled. "Well. Our work day is done. And we just need to be finished by the time dinner is ready, otherwise our boyfriend's twin will bust down the door and we'll get in trouble."

My laugh rang through the room as she came to the bed. My laugh whooshed into a gasp as she parted my legs.

"Are you sure you want to do this?" she whispered.

"Pris, I'm more sure of this than anything else in my entire life. Are you sure?"

"I am." She dragged me to the edge of the bed. "Red means stop."

I nodded eagerly. "Yellow means slow. Green means good."

"Good," she praised. "I like that you already know."

"I do," I whispered. "I'll do whatever you want me to do, Pris."

"So eager to please," she hummed. "What I want you to do right now is crawl to the saddle, lube it up, and show me how pretty your face looks while you come for me."

# 15
# priscilla

SKY DID EXACTLY as they were told.

They slid off the bed, their knees hitting the floor, pausing to look up at me with their pretty brown eyes. Their green hair was damp, a few water droplets clinging to their skin where the towel had missed them.

The way they looked up at me, the pure submission on their face—all of it stroked something deep and needy inside of me.

Sky crawled across the floor to the saddle. I sat on the edge of the bed, parting my thighs as I watched their every move. They opened the bottle of lube, poured some out in their hands, and stroked the dildo that was mounted to the saddle.

Fuck. I loved watching them get on their knees for me. I let out a soft hum, shaking my head as a wave of lust washed over me. I could sit here all day and watch them do this.

Their gaze occasionally flicked over to me, their expression mirroring the way I felt.

We'd both been dancing around our desires, and now, it

was finally happening. We were finally getting our time together.

I savored every second of watching them be so obedient, my heart pounding as Sky looked up at me. "Like this?" they asked.

I nodded. "Just like that. And when you're ready, I want you to get on."

They whimpered, their fingers sliding down to their pussy. "Oh God. I'm so wet."

I already *knew* that was the case. The two of us were so turned on from our shower and our time in the garden that I was pretty sure we were both fountains.

I slid my fingers down to my pussy and let out a soft moan, gliding them over my clit. "I am too," I huffed. "Watching you turns me on."

"Being watched by you turns *me* on," they answered.

A smirk crossed my lips and I stood up, crossing the room as they threw their leg over the saddle. I stepped up behind them and ran my fingers through the hair, gripping hard enough that they let out a soft, drawn out whine.

I loved the way their breath caught in their throat. I pulled their head back. Their lashes fluttered as their gaze locked with mine.

"I want you to take every single inch for me," I murmured.

"Yes, ma'am."

Their hips lifted as they guided the lubed toy to their entrance, a gasp parting their lips as they sank down.

*Heavenly*. That was the only word that came to mind as I watched them take it. I was in heaven.

My fingers tightened in their hair as they rocked their hips slowly, working the toy deeper. Their cheeks flushed, a dusty pink warm in their face as they began to move faster.

"Good," I praised. "Fuck, you look so good like this, little storm."

Their eyes lit up like lightning. "I love it when y'all call me that."

"It's the perfect nickname," I whispered.

The Sybian Saddle was one of my favorite sex toys for a multitude of reasons. It was one of the best toys I'd found for myself and for others too. There was something about riding it that always made my orgasms euphoric. Plus, I could switch out the toy attachments, depending on what I wanted.

And then there were the *vibrations*.

A big red button on the saddle was just waiting to be pushed. I pressed it and clamped my hand over Sky's mouth right before they cried out.

I wanted them all to myself right now, to do every single little thing I wanted to without any interruption. The last thing I wanted was for us to draw some attention from everyone on the ranch.

The vibrations hummed loudly, echoing through the bedroom. Sky's whimpers and moans were involuntary, and they were fighting for their life to stifle them. The vibrations intensified, their body bouncing on the saddle in a rhythm that was relentless. God, this was hot. I sucked in a breath, turned on as the sound of their pussy being pounded by the toy filled the room.

"Look at you," I purred. "So fucking helpless and needy right now, hmm?"

"Yes," they gasped. "I'm yours. All yours."

I kept my hand over their mouth as I leaned down to kiss their neck, reaching my other hand around to cup their breast and play with their nipples. I felt their teeth sink into my hand, a groan following as they were thrown straight to the edge.

This felt so fucking good. I loved being in control. They were so hot, so submissive and needy. They rode the saddle without hesitation while I teased them, their moans caught in my hands.

*Fuck.*

My pussy pulsed, begging to be touched. I needed relief as much as they did, my body tensing as shockwaves rippled across my skin. One hand continued to stifle the hot sounds they made, but my other went between my thighs, circling my clit.

"Oh god," I sighed.

I needed more. My body yearned for their touch. For their kiss.

I stepped around in front of them and leaned down, holding their gaze as I pressed the button to turn the vibration intensity.

"Fuck! *Fuck,*" they gasped, their head tossing back. "This is the best torture."

For both of us.

Their hands slid up the back of my thighs and dragged me forward. My palms settled on their head as they surprised me by burying their face against my pussy, their tongue circling my clit while they fucked themself on the saddle.

"Good," I gasped. "Fuck, that feels good."

I wanted their lips to be wet with my cum, the taste of us shared in our next kiss. Pleasure rippled through me, my mind blanking as they continued to lick me.

I could feel the vibrations rumbling through them passing through me now, too. We found a good tempo, both of our bodies moving as we chased pleasure.

This wasn't my first rodeo, and it wouldn't be the last. I wanted Sky to experience all the orgasms as they possibly could before they left Rainbow Ranch.

*If* they left.

I didn't want them to.

The longer I knew them, the more and more I wanted them to stay. But I didn't want to get my hopes up and be left with a broken heart.

Regardless, I wasn't going to miss the chance to be with them.

My knees felt like jelly. I drew them back and sank down, seating myself on the front part of the saddle, the constant vibrations rolling through every muscle as our bodies pressed together. Their arms wound around my neck, our lips meeting in a fevered kiss.

I could taste myself on them.

"You taste like me," I groaned.

I was so close. So fucking close.

Our bodies pressed closer, riding the saddle as one. Heat skated over my skin as I felt the teasing start of an orgasm.

"I'm almost there," they gasped.

"Me too, little storm," I panted.

I held onto them, kissing them hard as we rocked our hips together.

This was the kind of storm *I* liked to chase.

My orgasm crashed into me, my voice pitching as I came hard. Their body trembled, their head tossing back as they came too, both of us shaking as every nerve ending in our bodies lit up with all consuming pleasure.

My muscles melted, and my eyes flew open. I looked at them, right as their head tipped back, their lips glistening with my essence as they came hard a second time.

They were beautiful.

I memorized every line on their face, every line of their expression.

Something about seeing them on the saddle, our bodies pressed together, everything intertwined like rope—I'd never forget this time with them.

Sky's muscles went limp, and I turned off the saddle. We collapsed against each other, a tangled breathless mess.

"Wow," they whispered.

All I could do was nod after the strength of that climax.

They slowly lifted off the saddle, sinking to the floor as they panted. Before they got too settled there, I helped them stand, and led them to my bed, before tumbling onto the mattress together.

Somehow, they ended up on top of me—the solid weight of their body against mine grounding me. Their head settled between my breasts, and I stroked their hair as we both came down from the high of finally being in each other's arms.

"Am I a cowthey now?"

I barked out a laugh. "I'd say so. Am I a storm chaser?"

They giggled. "Yes. I'd say so."

I continued to stroke their back as we cuddled, my mind going blank.

For the first time in a while, I wasn't worried about doing anything wrong. Hell, I wasn't worried about anything. I simply enjoyed the moment, enjoyed the feeling of their body against mine. It was a special kind of bliss, one that I so rarely got to experience.

Eventually, my thoughts started to turn again. But the only thing I could think about was what else we could do together.

And what we could do together with Beau.

Sky lifted their head to look up at me, their cheeks still pink. "What are you thinking about?"

"I'm thinking about us and Beau," I said softly.

They let out a gentle hum. "Between the three of us, it seems like we'd have so much to explore. Especially given that we have a unique dynamic."

"Oh? And what dynamic is that?"

I liked the way they smirked. "You're dominant, he's a switch, and I'm submissive. *That* dynamic."

I grinned. "Oh, *that* one."

They were right though, the options were endless. I could command Beau to do things to them while I sat and watched, or participated.

"After the picnic, I was hoping the three of us could pursue those plans," I said.

Sky nodded. "I'd love that. I feel like you're already planning exactly what you're going to do to us."

They were right.

My mind was formulating all the wonderful kinky things we could do.

"You would be correct," I said.

Sky smiled, melting further against me.

The three of us together was all I was going to be thinking about until we got the chance to try.

# 16
# beau

Sunday morning rolled around before we knew it. And the good news was that despite the storm that had blown through overnight, the skies were bright blue and clear today. Puffy clouds drifted above, casting shadows down on the ranch as they passed by.

Our tents were up, our tables were set, blankets rolled out, activities ready to go. Pretty soon, every queer person in Oklahoma would be heading to our doorstep.

This was one of my favorite events of the year. And this year in particular, it felt special because we had Sky here with us.

Their first Pride. I loved that we got to share it with them.

Nothing could've prepared me for how quickly my life was changing.

For the better, too. I could see a future with Priscilla and Sky, one that was bright and full of possibilities. The idea of having two people who I could love forever had taken root, and I was doing my best to show them that I could be a good partner.

I knew I was good at being a boss.

Or at least, I tried.

I tried to do good by the people around me, always putting them first. It was something that my parents had taught me young, I was the oldest, and therefore I had all the responsibilities on my shoulders. And while I wasn't a lone cowboy, there were certainly some days where I felt like it.

But then Boone, Billie, and Benny reminded me I wasn't alone. We had each other, we had our friends, who were more like family anyhow.

Even knowing *that*, I still felt worried that I wasn't made to be a good partner. I was often up well before the crack of dawn, staying up late, always working. I would need to learn how to set aside time for those I loved, right? I wasn't sure how I was going to balance that quite yet, but I would do everything in my power to do it well.

The sound of boot steps behind me had me turning as my twin walked up. Boone raised his head to the sky, holding onto his hat as he tipped his head back.

"Perfect day for a picnic."

I slung my arm around his shoulders and smiled. "It is," I agreed.

He let out a hum in agreement, but I knew that hum. I raised a brow as I looked at him.

"Alright. Out with it," I said. "You're cooking up something in that head of yours."

"Oh you know," he chuckled. "Just wondering how everything is making you feel. I'm still caught up in the whirlwind of Wylie. I love him so much."

"I know you do," I said, leaning my head against his. "It's made me really damn happy to see the two of you together."

"I know. And it's made me happy to see you, Sky, and Pris together. The three of you seem like the perfect partners for each other."

I blew out a slow breath. "We haven't exactly labeled our relationship quite yet. I think . . ."

"Worried about Sky leaving?"

I nodded.

Of course he'd be able to read my mind. Our entire lives, we'd always known that the other was thinking. It was part of being brothers, being twins.

Boone knew me better than anyone.

"I worry I'm not good enough," I whispered.

Boone shook his head. "You gotta get that out of your mind, Beau. You deserve love. You deserve to feel the kind of happiness that makes you feel like you're floating in the clouds. It's special, what the three of you got."

I untangled myself from him and reached around, plucking my mask from my back pocket. I usually wore it for picnics and any official Rainbow Ranch event. It was something I picked up years ago and had stuck. I liked it, it made me feel like I was putting on a cape.

When the mask was on, I was Super Beau—able to handle anything and everyone around me.

"See," Boone said, nodding toward the tent. "Look at your partners working together. Sky belongs here."

"They aren't officially my partners yet," I grumbled.

"Sure," he said with a smirk. "It'll just be a matter of time, I'm sure. I should make a bet with Billie and Benny."

"You will do no such thing, Boone."

He chuckled and pecked my cheek. "I'm gonna go make sure all the food is being put out where I want it. Should I send Abilene to get Dennis?"

"Yes, please," I said.

It wouldn't be a Rainbow Ranch picnic without our unofficial mascot. Hopefully he behaved himself today.

Boone left my side to join everyone else under the tent. I turned and scouted the ranch, looking for anything that might be out of place. Rainbow flags whipped in the wind, the crops wavering as a breeze rolled through. Sunshine warmed me through my pastel plaid button-down and jeans.

My attention turned back to Pris and Sky. The two of them were setting up a couple more tables underneath one of the tents. Boone had joined Wylie and Winnie in getting the rest of the food and refreshments set out.

We were ready.

It was about time to grab my truck and head up to the front of the property to help direct people. While we had signs that we'd put up yesterday to guide people to the ranch, it never hurt to have someone at the front to welcome them in.

I rolled my shoulders and stretched my neck. I finally left my post and headed toward the tent, slowing as I approached. Everyone was working so well together. It was like watching magic happen right in front of me.

"I'm gonna head to the front," I said. "I'm gonna welcome people in."

"Sounds good," Boone said. "Why don't you take someone with you?"

I heard the knowing smirk in his voice.

"Don't you need the extra hands here?" I asked.

"You can take Sky," Pris said.

Sky shook their head. "How about you go?"

I saw mischief and their sweet brown eyes, and they winked at me before grabbing a cooler full of water. Pris smoothed her hands down her hips, and then shrugged her shoulders.

"Sure," she said. "I'll come with you."

She walked up to me and as she got close, the urge to pull her in and kiss her came over me.

I couldn't resist it.

Pris squeaked as I dragged her close to me. I swooped in, pressing my lips to hers before the whole ranch. Boone let out a low whistle and there were a couple of claps, because *of course* everyone was gonna be dramatic about it.

I let her go and half expected her to be scowling at me, but she was grinning ear to ear. My heart melted in my chest.

"Let's go welcome people in," I murmured.

She nodded and glanced back at Sky. "We'll be back for you in a bit, little storm. Can't miss your first Pride."

Sky's cheeks turned pink and they smirked. "Have fun."

———

A couple hours later, the Y'all Pride Picnic was in full swing, and I felt like I was on top of the world. I sat on a spread-out blanket next to Pris and Sky, the sun shining on the three of us as we chatted with some of the guests as they passed by or stopped to say hello.

I bit into a sandwich as I looked around. Everyone was having a good time as usual. Music floated on the breeze, the clouds drifting above us.

It was the perfect day on Rainbow Ranch.

Pris and I had worked the front gate for a little bit only to be relieved by Billie and Benny. We were taking a short break to eat and relax before getting back to helping out with all the other activities that were going on.

In about an hour, we would have an amazing drag performance, followed by Dennis making his famed appearance.

Sky leaned against me, resting their head on my shoulder.

"This is amazing," they sighed. "I didn't expect so many people to show up."

I smiled. Everyone here was comfortably themselves, and that type of vibe radiated warmth and happiness.

"It's one of my favorite events," I said. "I always feel good about what we do here."

"You should," Pris chimed. "Rainbow Ranch is a safe place in a state that isn't always safe—and that's important."

"It's a sanctuary," Sky said. "I'm happy to be here."

*Will you stay?* The question almost tumbled out, but I bit my bottom lip. Pris glanced over at me, and I wondered if she'd almost said the same thing.

The three of us were dancing around the tension. After the picnic, I wondered if we'd finally get to test the waters of being together.

Falling for two people certainly hadn't been on my plan for this year, but here I was.

My heart told me I loved them both, even if it was too fast. But Sky was like a tornado that had torn through our lives, leaving in its wake a desire for something more.

"We need to get you your own hat," Pris said to Sky. "Especially after all that riding you did yesterday."

My eyes widened. "Did you ride one of the horses yesterday? Did I miss that?"

They both burst out laughing.

"Not that kind of riding, Beau," Pris said, giving my thigh a squeeze.

"*Oh.*"

I blushed, and then smirked, looking down at Sky.

I did the only thing I could think of. I grabbed my cowboy hat, lifted it off my head, and placed it on theirs.

A couple whistles followed, because of course there was some significance in giving someone a hat.

In a way, I was marking them as mine.

Sky blushed, giving me a quick kiss on the cheek.

And then Priscilla shocked us both by lifting her hat, leaning over, and placing it on my head.

Now it is my turn to blush, and I grinned from ear to ear, my cheeks turning red beneath my mask.

"There," she said. "You look damn good in my hat, Beau Adams."

"Well, you'll look good in my—" I cut myself off before I said something inappropriate in front of the entire world.

"No, no," she giggled. "Go ahead and finish that sentence."

"I don't think I will," I said, my ears now burning.

Sky and Priscilla burst into another fit of giggles, the two of them teasing me.

But it felt really damn good to be teased like this. It felt even better to be with them.

Now Sky was wearing my hat, I was wearing Priscilla's, and everything in the world felt right.

But then there was the tension between us. It was driving me just a little crazy. Last night, I'd even dreamed about them.

Even out in the open, there was this boiling heat between us that was eating me alive. All I could think about was what it would be like for the three of us to finally get to explore our dynamics together.

I needed to confirm what I knew to be true.

We belonged together.

What would it be like?

Priscilla leaned against me and left a kiss on my cheek before getting up. She smoothed her hands down her jeans and adjusted her button-down shirt. When she turned, I noticed a stitched heart on a leather patch.

"I love those jeans," I said.

She tossed a smile over her shoulder and patted her ass. "I bet you do. I'm gonna go help out your family. Break time is over."

I nodded, letting out a long sigh. "It's time for me to get up too, I need to wrangle Dennis."

"I'm going to hand out more food," Sky said.

"But," Priscilla said. "After the picnic . . ."

I swallowed hard. "After the picnic, I think that we should meet at my door."

Both of them nodded in agreement.

"Sounds like a date," Pris said.

"It sure does," Sky agreed.

# 17
# sky

AFTER THE Y'ALL Pride Picnic, we helped clean everything up. The picnic was a complete whirlwind success and I was already excited for the next one. Experiencing Pride for the first time on Rainbow Ranch had meant more to me than there were words to express.

But, before we could get caught up in another project—the three of us excused ourselves and met at Beau's door. Tension crackled in the air. Lust had been building between us throughout the entire day, my heart pounding with excitement.

Beau smirked at the two offs. "Fancy meeting you both here."

"Beau," Pris snorted. "Open the damn door."

"Yes, ma'am."

He opened it and stepped through, Pris and I tumbling in after him. I wasn't sure if this would be awkward initially, but now I had the answer as Pris tugged me into a hungry kiss.

Beau's hands settled on my hips. I melted against Pris, whimpering as I ended up between the two of them.

"Is this okay?" he asked.

"Yes," I gasped. God, it was more than okay. I'd been dreaming about this every night since coming to Rainbow Ranch. "The two of you can do whatever you want to me. I've been thinking about this for so long now. I need you. *Both* of you."

Beau leaned down, slowly kissing my neck. He was still wearing his mask from the picnic. It was hot. *Really* fucking hot. Shivers of need rolled up my spine, my mind already spinning toward subspace. Pris ran her hands up my body, pausing once she came to the belt buckle.

The metal clinked as his lips brushed my skin, the belt slowly pulled off.

The tension in the room made my heart squeeze. I gasped, my head falling back against Beau's hard chest as more waves of pleasure rolled through me.

"I've been needing this," Beau grunted.

"Me too, cowboy," Pris sighed. "I like watching you kiss them. I like listening to all those beautiful little noises they make, too."

*Oh.* I could just come from listening to her voice and the way she talked to us. The gentle dominance that made me want to get on my knees and beg for more.

"Do we need to pause and talk?" Beau asked. "I know we know most of each other's kinks, but . . ."

Pris swallowed hard and nodded, taking a step back. "That's a good idea."

"Damn," I whined, but they were probably right. We had been building up to this moment for so long, but communication was always important. "I will do whatever you want me to."

Pris wrinkled her nose. "Not *whatever*, I'm sure."

"You'd be surprised," I said, making Beau chuckle.

"I think we should take it slow," Pris said. "I think we should feel it out together. I'll tell Beau what to do, with his consent, and we'll go from there. I like the idea of using some rope, too."

"Me too," he said. "I like the idea of dominating Sky at your command, but then submitting to you."

Pris nodded. "I like that idea, too."

"I'll get the ropes," he said. "So we have them. I have experience using rope."

"Oh, I know. I've seen you compete at the rodeo plenty of times."

"You compete?" I asked in surprise.

He nodded, planting a kiss on the top of my head before heading to a dresser beneath the window in his room. He opened it and pulled out bundles of rope.

"I'm good at lassoing," he said.

"Oh really?" I asked.

He raised a brow at us, and then let one of the rope bundles drop with practiced ease. My eyes widened as he created a loop, and I yelped as it flew across the bedroom around Pris and I, pulling us together. Pris laughed as the rope tightened and he dragged us toward him, kissing her hard on the mouth and then me.

"I take back my teasing," I croaked.

Pris smirked. "You'll get to watch our cowboy show off at the rodeo."

Beau winked and let the ropes drop, gathering them and placing them on the bed.

"I feel good about all that's been discussed," he said.

"I do too," I agreed.

Pris nodded. "Me too. Okay then." She clapped her hands together, her eyes dancing with a hint of mischief. "I want you to touch them, Beau. Unbutton their shirt and tease them until they're making all those pretty sounds."

"Yes, ma'am," Beau said.

He tugged me closer, tipping my chin up. I smiled up at him, enjoying his soft chuckle as he leaned down and kissed me hard.

Beau let out a moan, his rough hands sliding across my chest. He slowly unbuttoned my shirt, exposing the binder I wore underneath. It compressed my breasts, flattening them against my chest.

The shirt landed in a heap on the floor, and he carefully lifted my binder away, exposing me completely. My nipples were already hard, and all of the heat between us made my pussy pulse.

"Fuck," I whispered. "You feel so good, Beau."

"You feel even better," he murmured.

His voice was deep, his Southern accent making it rougher. He cupped my breast, rolling my nipples between his thumb and forefinger. I gasped, my eyelashes fluttering as I looked up at Pris. She grabbed my chin, forcing me to hold her gaze as he continued to tease me.

"Just like that," she murmured. "Keep watching me with those stormy eyes. I love it when you look like that."

"Pris," I breathe out. "This feels so good."

"I know it does. Keep teasing them," she instructed Beau.

While he continued to tease me, she slowly unbuttoned my jeans, the zipper rolling down. My hips bucked as she pulled the fabric down, taking the black boxers I had underneath with them.

I sucked in a breath as I helped kick out of the rest of my clothing, followed by my boots and then my socks.

Now I was completely naked between the two of them.

Pris grabbed hold of Beau's arm, guiding him until he stood behind me, his body pressing against mine. He rested his chin on my shoulders, occasionally peppering kisses over my skin as he kept playing with me.

Pris ran her hands down the front of my thighs, shoving them apart. I groaned as she leaned forward, her tongue flicking against my clit.

"Fuck," I whimpered.

Tiny shocks of pleasure burst through me. There wasn't another place in the world I'd rather be than between the two of them.

"Lift their leg," Pris demanded.

Beau leaned down, catching my leg in his arm and lifting. I was off balance, falling back against him, but he wasn't going to let me go anywhere.

And now my pussy was even more exposed to her. I whimpered, my head spinning as I started to tumble into the headspace I loved. I trusted both of them to take care of me, to use me however they pleased.

I trusted them.

"Fuck," he grunted. "The two of you look so good."

Pris sank to her knees, surprising me. My head thrashed as she began to work me with her tongue, brushing two fingers against my entrance.

I was already soaked.

Now that I was finally getting to be with them, I was satisfying the deep curiosity that had been plaguing me for the last week.

What would it be like to be with them? Now I was finding out the truth—and it was everything I dreamed of and more.

All the pleasure rolling through my body was because of how they treated me with such care and desire.

I couldn't remember the last time I'd ever been touched like this—if ever.

Two fingers dipped inside, drawing a whimper from me as Beau continued to kiss up and down my neck. Soft shivers rose through my body, electricity skating over my skin.

They were both taking it slow, their movements mirroring each other. Driving me crazy just by taking their sweet time. It was just as hot as the rush of being fucked hard and fast, but more torturous.

She thrust her fingers inside me, finding that spot that was bound to make me come fast. I gasped as her lips fit around my clit, sucking gently.

"Are you going to come for Pris?" Beau whispered. "Are you going to be good for her?"

"Yes," I whined. "I-I want to be good."

Pris drew back for a moment. "I can't wait to taste your sweet orgasm on my tongue, Sky. You're going to be so good for us and come, aren't you?"

"Yes," I rasped.

I was already on the edge. All of the sensations rolling over me overwhelmed me in the best way possible. I arched back against him, my hands reaching up to loop behind his neck. He continued to pinch and tease my nipples, all while her tongue worked magic on my pussy.

"Yes, yes, yes," I gasped. "Please. Please let me come. *Please.*"

Beau pinched one of my nipples harder. "You sound mighty fine when you're begging."

*Fuck.* Just hearing him say that sent me over the edge. His hand clamped over my mouth to stifle my scream, so we didn't draw attention from anyone in the rest of the house.

I came hard, her tongue still lapping me up, catching

every drop. She pulled her fingers out of me, her tongue still circling my clit until my orgasm ebbed.

I melted against Beau, panting hard. I was seeing stars.

Pris stood up. She reached past me, offering the fingers that had just been inside me to Beau. He parted his lips and sucked them, a low growl leaving him.

"Don't they taste like heaven?" she asked.

"They sure do," he growled. "I want more."

"We'll get more," Pris promised.

I was limp, every muscle completely relaxed. She leaned forward, brushing her lips against mine. I could taste myself on them. Beau slowly let my leg down. I felt a bulge behind me, the shape of his erection pressing against my ass.

She winked at us, taking a step back and grabbing a bundle of rope from the bed. Safety shears gleamed next to the other bundle, ready to be used in case we needed them.

Beau continued to stroke my body up and down, the occasional wave of need rolling back through me, even though I'd just come for them.

"I want to be in a chest harness," I whispered.

"Oh, I know," Pris said. "And then you're going to help me put our cowboy in a chest harness too."

"Me?" he asked.

"Yes, you," she said. "If you want, of course."

"I would love to," he said. "I don't think I've ever actually been put in a chest harness before."

"Oh," I said, looking up at him, and then Pris. "We should do him first."

She nodded in agreement. "I think so too."

As much as I wanted to be in a harness, the idea of seeing him tied up for the first time was far more exciting.

"What do I do?" Beau asked.

"You can start by kneeling for us," Pris answered.

He went down to his knees without a question asked. My eyes widened as she circled us, slowly unraveling the rope as her gaze traced us.

"Both of you are so obedient," she said. "And now I get to have Sky help tie you up. How does it feel to know that you're submitting to me?"

"It feels really damn good," he whispered.

"Sky, I want you to undress him."

"Yes ma'am," I said immediately.

I turned to face him and then slowly reached up to remove his mask.

"Leave the mask," she said.

I nodded, offering him a smile before running my hands over his shoulders. Even on his knees, he was very tall. I undid the top button of his shirt, and then the second, and the third. I made my way down until his chest was completely exposed, and I could tug it away and add to the heap of clothing that belonged to me.

His eyes danced behind the mask in the moonlight filling the bedroom, his breath catching as he looked me up and down. I paused to lean forward, brushing my mouth against him in a reassuring kiss.

I knew just how vulnerable it was to be submissive. You had to build trust with the person you were putting yourself in that position with. And even with having safe words and rules in place, it was still a completely new experience to submit so wholeheartedly for me.

It was beautiful, heartwarming, erotic. But it was also sharing the part of your soul that was most tender and raw.

I got down to my knees, unbuckling his belt and tugging it. The leather slid over denim, snapping as it came free. I popped his jeans open and we worked together to get them off his body.

Now both of us were naked.

His cock was hard. My eyes widened as I looked down at him.

"May I touch you?" I asked.

"Yes. *Please.*"

I circled his cock with my hand, giving him a stroke from base to tip. His head fell back, his throat bobbing as Pris stepped up behind him, making a loop of rope around his torso.

Pris gave his shoulder a light tap. "Stand up. Sky, I want you to stay on your knees."

He got back up to his feet, his cock right in front of my face. My mouth watered. I parted my lips and leaned forward, taking the head over his cock into my mouth. He let out the longest groan.

"Fuck," he whimpered.

Truly, there was something about hearing a tough man whimper that changed my brain in chemistry.

One thing that always turned me on was pleasing someone else, and watching his face twist in pleasure as I sucked him felt so damn good. I circled the base of his cock, stroking him as I bobbed my head up and down.

The sounds he made turned me on even more, all while Pris continued to move around him, slowly tying a harness around his body. Directing him, moving his arms, putting the two of us in even more of a submissive space.

This was one of my favorite things about BDSM, especially if I was playing with more than one person. The energy shared in the room and the way we work together was beautiful. Threads in a tapestry of desire and lust, all crossing together to create a bigger picture.

The salty taste of him sat on my tongue, my eyes rolling back as I took him deeper. He hit the back of my throat, his hips giving a light thrust as the ropes vibrated over each other.

Pris continued to work the rope, and every time I looked up, he had more binding his body. His cheeks were flushed, his eyes feasting on me while I was on my knees for him.

She gave him a light hug, and leaned forward, kissing his neck. I continued to suck his cock, feeling him shiver as we drove him closer to the edge.

Were we going to be able to make him come? It was my favorite kind of challenge. I wanted him to come. I wanted to taste him.

I wanted to give him the same satisfaction he'd given me.

I drew back to catch my breath for a moment. "Please come for me," I whispered. "I want to taste you. I want you to fuck my throat."

"Did you hear them?" Pris asked. "They want you to fuck their throat."

"Are you sure?" he rasped.

"Of course," I said. "Please, Beau. I need it. Use me. Fuck my mouth."

His fingers gripped the top of my hair and he yanked me forward. Surprise rolled through me as his cock shoved into my mouth, all the way to the back of my throat.

The euphoria returned at full blast, rumbling through my body as he held me in place, using me the way that I wanted him to. I felt so damn good to be fucked like this.

The sound of his cock gliding in and out of my mouth and hitting the back of my throat, our bodies slapping together. I heard Pris move around us, and then felt her hands on my shoulders as she sank down behind me. Her nails raked down my back, leaving a streak of pain that made me wet all over again.

His hips snapped harder, thrusting in and out. I choked around his cock, my body pressing against hers. Her hand snaked up the front of my body, clasping around my throat gently.

I could stay here forever.

Worshiping them. *Obeying* them.

A low growl left him, and I knew that he was getting close. It was evident in the way that he moved, the way that his grip tightened in my hair. I moaned as he gave one final thrust, heat bursting down my throat. He came hard and fast, and I swallowed every single drop.

He slowly drew back, panting hard. The taste of his cum sat on my tongue, leaving me with a deep-rooted satisfaction that I had pleased him.

"You both did so well for me," Pris praised.

My head was spinning. I turned, catching her mouth against mine.

She kissed me hard, dragging me against her as our tongues explored each other's mouths. The taste of him was shared between us, my hands gliding up her body.

As I reached for her, fabric was rough beneath my hands, reminding me she was still dressed.

"Can we undress you?" I asked.

"Let us please you," Beau pleaded.

We were both eager to make her come, too.

"Yes," she said. "Take me to the bed."

Beau lifted her with ease, carrying her to the bed. He plopped her down at the center, and the two of us climbed onto the mattress, working together to undress her quickly.

Moonlight poured in through the window, filling up the bedroom, as if a light were on. It lit up our bodies, catching her hard nipples and glistening pussy. I glanced over at Beau. He was so unbelievably hot in his mask and harness.

I had to be the luckiest person alive.

I kissed up her calf, and then her thigh, slowing as I neared her pussy. She spread her legs for me, her eyes fluttering.

He leaned over her, their lips brushing each other as her hand closed around his cock. I pressed a kiss to her pussy and then circled her clit with my tongue.

The three of us pleased each other. I slid my hand down to my pussy, realizing how wet I still was. Drenched from coming so hard, and then from everything we'd done tonight so far.

He let out a long groan, drawing back for a second as his cock hardened.

"Ready for a second round?" she teased.

"You know, between the two of you, I'll be hard all night," he huffed.

I laughed, and then slid two fingers inside her slowly. Her pussy felt like silk, her muscles milking me.

"How does she feel?" he asked.

"So fucking good," I whispered.

I started to pull my hand away, but Pris shook her head.

"Don't you dare stop now, Sky."

I grinned and lowered my mouth to her pussy again. "Yes, ma'am."

# 18
# priscilla

MY BACK ARCHED as Beau and Sky worked together to please me. I moaned as Sky thrust their fingers in and out of me while Beau kissed and sucked my nipples. My entire body vibrated with pleasure, but I needed more.

The dynamics we'd set up initially melted away, a level of intuition sinking between the three of us that felt natural. It felt right.

"I want you inside me, Beau," I gasped.

He groaned. "Fuck."

"Do it," Sky rasped. "I want to be beneath her while you fuck her."

"Yes," Beau said immediately.

He lifted me with ease. In one swift motion, I ended up on all fours, my ass facing him. Beau paused for a moment to grab a condom, ripping the foil and rolling it on quickly. I whimpered as his rough palms ran up my back and then back down to my hips, grabbing hold of them. I pushed Sky down beneath me, the two of us kissing.

Our legs tangled as we adjusted our bodies, figuring out the best position to make this happen in.

"This feels good," Sky gasped.

I kissed down their neck and then gave them a light shove, moving them up the bed until my face hovered above their pussy. I felt the head of his cock against me and pushed back, feeling him enter me.

"Fuck," we groaned together.

His grip on my hips tightened, and he pushed forward, filling me all the way to the hilt.

My cry echoed through the room. Sky put their hand over my mouth, their eyes widening.

"That was loud," they giggled.

"Fuck it," I rasped. "We need to get some soundproof walls in this place."

Beau let out a dark laugh. "I'll add it to the top of my to-do list."

It was impossible to stay completely quiet. And at this point, I wasn't even sure if I cared if anyone heard us.

Beau leaned over, trailing kisses down my spine as he began to drive in and out. My pussy gripped him hard, adjusting to the size of him with every thrust.

"That feels so good," I said, shaking my head as I fought the urge to be louder.

My breasts rubbed against Sky's body, their skin soft against mine. My face hovered right above their pussy, the scent of their sex making my mouth water. Sensations after sensation rippled through me, sending aching shivers up and down my spine.

Being with the two of them felt so perfectly good. I'd been anticipating this for so long, and now that I have them together, it was everything that I dreamed of and more.

Putting Beau into the rope while Sky sucked him off had turned me on in so many different ways. I looked over my shoulder, my eyes widening as I took him in. His mask added another layer of mystery to our hot, humble cowboy. The red rope created a harness around his broad, tanned chest.

"You're so hot," I whimpered.

He gave a breathless smile as the sound of our skin slapping together picked up in rhythm. The bed squeaked beneath us and I fought a laugh at the thought of us breaking the bed frame.

"Beau," I groaned. "Is your bed going to hold up?"

"If it doesn't, then I'll make a new one," he huffed, fucking me harder.

Sky laughed, and then their laugh melted into a long gasp as I turned my attention on them. I held their gaze as I lowered my mouth to their pussy, the taste of them sweet and salty on my tongue. I glided the tip of my tongue over their clit and then lower, pushing their thighs back and folding them in half as I drove inside of them.

"Yes," they whined. "Please don't stop. That feels so good."

I couldn't get enough of them. I worked my tongue in and out of them until my jaw ached, and even then I wasn't going to stop. I wasn't going to stop until they were a quivering little mess for us.

Beau's cock hit deeper and I gasped. His moans and grunts matched Sky's, creating my favorite kind of song. He was hitting the perfect spot, gliding over my G-spot and sending shockwaves through me.

The three of us fell into a rhythm that was heated and everything we'd been needing since Sky showed up on our doorstep. He fucked me harder, every stroke pushing me closer to the edge. We were all chasing our orgasms and pleasure together, and that felt so damn right.

My fingers replaced my tongue, moving in and out of

Sky. Their voice pitched louder and I sucked in a breath, watching their uninhibited display of passion as I felt them start to tremble.

"Come for us," I demanded. "Come for me, little storm. You can do it. You look so damn pretty when you come."

Between my encouragement and praise, their hips bucked and I felt them clench around my fingers as they came for us.

I'd never get tired of making them orgasm.

"God, look at them," Beau huffed, pausing in his thrusts to admire our partner.

"Isn't that hot?" I murmured.

Sky let out a sound halfway between a groan and laugh, their body trembling as they rode out their orgasm. I pulled my fingers free and sucked them, enjoying the taste that was Sky's pleasure.

Beau leaned over me, his arms wrapping around my body as he started to pump into me again. His cock drove in and out, his hands cupping my breasts and teasing my nipples. One slid down to my pussy, two fingers resting against my clit and circling as he continued to take me.

There was no way I was gonna last long at this rate. I was already so close to the edge from the constant teasing.

"I can't wait to feel you come on my cock," Beau groaned.

"Damn it," I rasped.

Hearing him say that unlocked something inside me. I pushed my ass back to meet his thrusts, whimpering as he kept going. Sky moved out from beneath me and readjusted themselves, sliding back under me with their head down below so they could see him fucking me. I gasped as they pulled his hand away from my clit, replacing it with their tongue.

I rested my head against their pussy as Beau's fingers dug into my hips, his moan following.

"I'm close," he huffed.

All I could do was whimper.

"Fuck," he grunted again.

The three of us moaned together. Sky's tongue flicked against my clit and a wave of pleasure rose up, my head lifting as I felt the edge of my climax.

Fuck. I was there. I gasped, my head tossing back as I came hard, my orgasm consuming every single part of me.

"Yes, yes," I groaned, my body shaking through my climax.

Beau pulled out of me quickly and I looked back, moving slightly so that he could offer the head of his cock to Sky.

"Give it to me," they begged. "Please. I want every single drop."

Damn. *That* was hot.

Sky pulled the condom free and took him down their throat right as he came, his head tipping back on a long groan. My entire body buzzed as I watched, still riding the euphoric high of my own orgasm as I watched the two people I wanted most in the world please each other, too.

Sky swallowed, their throat moving with every pump. I moved off them, collapsing to the side as Beau pulled back, cum glistening on their lips.

"I want a taste," I rasped, dragging them into an open mouthed kiss.

Sky relaxed into me, the taste of Beau's cum shared between us. There was something so deeply satisfying about tasting his release, the saltiness of it making me lick my lips as I drew back.

He collapsed on the other side of the bed next to us. Sky

ended up in the middle and they rolled onto their back, breathing hard.

"That was . . ." Beau trailed off. "That was amazing."

"It was," Sky panted.

I held up a thumbs up, earning a couple of chuckles.

"And yet, there's still so much I want to try," Beau said.

"Me too," I whispered.

I blinked a few times and then raised my head to look over at him. "Need me to take off your harness?"

"Soon," he said, turning over onto his side. His arm looped over Sky and settled on me, pulling the two of us into a hug. "But not yet. This is comfortable."

It was.

I smiled to myself and found my eyes slowly drifting closed.

I wanted this to be how I fell asleep every night.

With a smile on my face, in the arms of the two people I loved.

# 19
# sky

IN A RARE MOMENT of cell service, my phone's weather radar alert went off in the middle of the night, jolting me awake.

I was sandwiched between Pris and Beau, the three of us somehow squeezed together on his bed. I grabbed my phone and silenced it before it woke either one of them, glancing side to side.

Pris and Beau were both snoring softly. I smiled to myself, a feeling of content washing over me. Last night was something special. The connection between the three of us was deeply rooted. All of the feelings that had been swirling through me since I came here had proven to be right.

I swallowed hard and opened my phone, my eyes widening as I saw the weather alert.

A storm cell was brewing a few miles north of us, and it looked promising. They were predicting a couple of tornadoes, both estimated to be E2s. I checked my emails while I had a strong connection, and saw one from the organization I did some work for.

They were asking for more footage and data if I could make it out there.

I felt a streak of excitement over what I knew best—chasing storms, taking photos, gathering data. It was in my blood, this desire to learn everything I possibly could about them.

I went back to the radar, pressing my lips together as I studied the pattern.

There'd hardly been any storms, except for the day I'd come to Rainbow Ranch.

Did I wake them and let them know I was going out?

I knew Beau would be nervous if I did. And even more so if I brought Pris with me.

I chewed my bottom lip and then decided to hell with it. I'd go track the storms and see if I got anything. More than likely, I wouldn't. Storms were so unpredictable, and most fizzled out before becoming anything dangerous.

Carefully, I slid out of bed and quietly redressed. My muscles were a little sore, but the ache was the good kind. I brushed my fingers across the rope marks around my torso and smiled to myself.

I liked seeing the aftermath of being together. They reminded me of everything we'd shared.

Today was the day I needed to tell them I wanted to stay.

I wanted Rainbow Ranch to be my home.

I wanted to keep chasing the love I felt for both of them.

*Love.*

My heart beat faster as the realization washed over me completely.

I loved both of them.

My eyes pricked with tears. I'd been dreaming of feeling

this way my entire life, but now that I felt it—it was scary. Was I even good enough for them? Could they love me back? Was I moving too fast?

A whole flood of doubts rushed over me as I backed to the door, quietly stepping out. The moment the door clicked softly behind me, I took off down the hallway to my bedroom and went in, snatching my backpack and keys. I caught a glimpse of the clock on my bedside table.

It was five a.m., which gave me plenty of time to chase the storm, and meant the sun might rise in time to light up the pictures.

It also gave me plenty of time to wonder what the hell I was doing.

I was so sure Rainbow Ranch was the place for me. I knew it was. But it still suddenly felt scary to think about being here.

I rushed down the hall and through the living room, quietly stepping out onto the front porch. The barn lights cut through the darkness, but in the distance I could see the bands of lightning dancing in a wall of clouds.

"There you are," I whispered.

The rush of exhilaration hit me and all my other worries disappeared. I jogged down the steps and headed to the garage, pulling the massive door open. I hopped in my van, tossed my backpack in the passenger seat, and cranked on the engine.

The van rumbled to life. I flipped on the headlights and sat still for a moment.

I should have left a note that I was going to chase a storm. But, I'd be back before they woke up, especially since it was so close.

I pulled out of the garage, the tires crunching over the

gravel as I soared down the road past the arena and toward the front of the property.

Within a few minutes, I pulled up to the gate and hopped out, pushing it open so I could drive through. I realized this was the first time I'd left the ranch since arriving, and I paused, looking back at it.

A sense of calm settled over me and I smiled to myself.

This was meant to be. I was supposed to be here. I knew that so deeply, that my eyes watered up.

"See you again soon," I whispered.

Getting back in the van, I peeled out onto the road, took a right, and floored it straight toward the storm.

The van was my pride and joy. The console had the primary computer, a touchscreen monitor, power equipment, radar, and GPS that allowed me route plan efficiently. The radar helped me keep up to date with the storm and allowed me to make educated guesses on which way it may turn.

Without an assistant, it was a little tough, but I could do this. I'd done it a thousand times before. I'd been hunting storms for years.

I rushed through a curtain of rain, and the downpour started. I kicked up my wipers to the highest setting as lightning shot across the sky, the visibility on the road less than ideal. I glanced over at the radar, my eyes widening.

This one was heating up fast.

I slowed as the rain turned harsher, rolling down the empty country road. The storm was moving southeast, which meant I needed to find another road that could pull me closer.

"Come on, come on," I murmured. "*There* it is."

I spotted a smaller offshoot of a road and took the turn,

hydroplaning for a split second before the van righted itself. I barreled down the road, hitting a few spots of mud.

The downside of being out in the middle of nowhere was the rough roads, but that wasn't going to stop me. This van was built to handle a lot.

Way off in the distance, a break in the clouds gave way to a patch of emerging sun, the sky a hazy purple. If I got lucky, there'd be just enough light to get some good photos.

"Come on, come on," I said.

My heart was racing. I sped down the road, glancing out the window, back to the radar, then to the GPS.

I was going off instinct at this point. My gut twisted as I took a left down another small road, barreling past fields of corn.

This was going to be a good spot. I slowed and pulled off the side of the road as the rain slowed, the sky rumbling above. Lightning danced, streaking through dark clouds.

I pulled out into the field. The moment I stopped, I got out and opened the side door, rummaging through my bags. I pulled on a bright yellow rain poncho and yanked the hood up, then got out my camera.

When I glanced over my shoulder, I could see the clouds swirling in the distance.

I was going to get lucky.

My veins buzzed with excitement and a bit of fear. There was always danger in this job, but I knew when I needed to get the hell out of dodge.

With my camera set up, I climbed inside and looked at the GPS, mentally making a note of a couple of escape routes. If the storm came toward me, I'd be able to backtrack the way I'd come. Or I could take a road that would dart straight in front of it, but if I moved fast enough I'd be out of its path.

Plan in place, I hopped out of the van and waded through the tall grass, looking up at the sky.

It was coming.

Thunder shook the entire world.

I held up my camera, snapping a few shots as the storm formed in the distance, the funnel swirling as it reached for the land. It would be an EF2 at the very least, based on the predictions and the radar, but I was safely far enough that I wasn't too worried about being in the line of fire.

Rain started up again and pelted the poncho I wore, my camera shuttering as I snapped more photos. The wind whipped around me, smothering the tall grass of the field.

"Wow," I whispered, watching in awe.

It was a terrible, formidable, awe-inspiring part of nature. It was incredible to be on the ground and see something so powerful and destructive form right before my eyes.

There was beauty in its power, but it carried with it a sadness. I thought about the storm that tore up the small town I'd grown up in. I thought about all of the people whose lives were changed forever because of storms like this.

That's why I chased them.

Any data I could contribute to the scientists at the organization I worked for would eventually help improve our storm warning systems. It would help people be able to get to safety sooner.

I took more photos and then frowned, my gaze drawn by something else in the sky.

"No way," I whispered.

Another funnel was forming. My mouth dropped as I kept the shutter going, simultaneously taking video as I watched it form.

Twins. Twin tornadoes.

A shiver rolled up my spine as the clouds dropped rapidly, that funnel forming so fast that every part of my being told me to leave.

I lowered my camera, my eyes widening.

It was going in a different direction than the other.

It was coming straight toward me.

Which meant it was heading for Rainbow Ranch, too.

Adrenaline kicked in and I rushed to the van, slamming the doors shut and tossing my things into the front seat. The air went still—eerie—as I started the van, my heart pounding as the sound, which could only be described as a freight train, started to grow louder.

I slammed my foot on the pedal, peeling out of the field and onto the paved road.

*Fuck, fuck, fuck.* I'd memorized the road on the way to this spot, but now racing back, going over eighty in a van like this, sent a streak of worry through me. I glanced in the rearview, seeing the mass of swirling debris and wind chasing me. I had a head start, but I needed to get out of its path.

I needed to get home to Pris and Beau.

I needed to get home to Rainbow Ranch.

# 20
# beau

THUNDER SHOOK me from my sleep. My eyes flew open and in the dark, I could see the outline of Pris.

But not Sky.

I frowned and sat up, looking around the room. Lightning flashed bright enough that it lit up the room.

My chest twisted as my thoughts started to race. Thunder shook the entire house and all of the alarm bells rang in my head. I reached over, giving Priscilla a gentle shake.

She immediately turned over, lifting her head. "What's wrong?"

"I'm sorry to wake you up, darling," I whispered. "Did Sky tell you they were going somewhere?"

She shook her head and then sat up, looking up at the ceiling as the sound of rain became torrential.

"Fuck," she whispered. "Do you think . . ."

"That they left us?" My throat squeezed. There was no way, right?

Suddenly I worried that I'd moved too fast with them.

Priscilla's eyes widened in the dark. "No, Beau. I don't

think they did. Not after last night. Could they have gone outside to look at the storm?"

"Maybe. I don't like this," I said.

"Me neither. Let's find them," she said.

Lightning flashed again as we both got out of bed, quickly throwing on our clothes. I heard boots out in the hallway and my door flew open, Benny poking his head in.

"Oh god—"

"We're dressed," Pris said quickly. "What's wrong?"

"This storm is bad," he said. "We're all getting up."

"We're up," I said. "Let's go out and secure the stables if we have time."

He nodded and took off. My heart skipped a beat as I looked over at Pris. "I have to go help. You should grab Winnie and Boone and head to the storm shelter."

"I'm going to find Sky," she said, her eyes blazing with determination.

"Just be careful," I said. "I'll keep an eye out for them."

She rushed over to me, grabbed me by my face, and planted a kiss on my mouth. "You be careful, too," she said. "Go."

I nodded and left the bedroom, rushing down the hall and knocking on any door that was shut. The last one was Billie, and I kicked it open without warning.

"Get up," I called. "There's a storm."

She sat up in bed with a curse and then scrambled up, kicking into emergency mode. "I'm up," she said. "Fuck. Tornado?"

"Maybe. We're going out to secure the stables, but everyone else should head to the shelter."

"Got it," she said, already pulling on her boots. "Be careful."

"I will."

I ran through the house and out the front door.

The rain was pouring, but I didn't care. The ranch always came first.

Come hell or high water, flood or fire—the ranch always came first.

We had to make sure our horses were going to be okay. I sprinted across the road, looking around for Sky. I glanced back at the garage, noting that the door was open.

*Goddamnit.* They'd gone storm chasing.

The idea of them being out there alone in this sent a streak of fear a mile wide through me.

What if they got hurt? What if something went wrong?

I forced myself to breathe.

I had to trust that they knew what they were doing. Sky wasn't new to storm chasing. They wouldn't do something to purposefully put themself in harms way.

But I worried.

I worried because I loved them.

"Beau! We need help!" Benny shouted.

My attention was drawn back to the storm and the task at hand. I went through the gate and ran as fast as I could to the stables. We needed to get the doors chained, and everything secured.

Wylie, Benny, and I worked fast.

The horses neighed, stomping the ground nervously as the wind howled outside.

Whenever a bad storm hit, the best we could do was hunker down, and the stables were by far the strongest building we had on the property.

As humans could get down into a storm shelter, but our animals? We put all our money into making sure our stables were as secure as possible during a storm.

"Beau!" Wylie yelled.

I turned back as I secured one of the doors. "What?"

"Dennis got out!"

*Fuck.* "Dammit," I rasped, securing the chains.

The sound of rain and thunder grew louder. The wind was battering the stables, the horses uneasy.

"I'll get him," I yelled. "Finish securing everything and get to the shelter!"

Wylie and Benny nodded. The three of us were drenched from the rain. I raked my fingers through my hair and went back out the front, holding my arm over my head as I scouted the ranch.

Where in the hell had Dennis gone? Where was he?

"Dennis!" I shouted.

The damn troublemaker. I loved that little menace and didn't want anything to happen to him.

Headlights flashed and my head whipped back as I spotted Sky's van. Relief flooded through me, but then it was followed by a wave of pure panic and fear.

Behind them, in the distance, was a twister.

Heading straight for our ranch.

"Get to the shelter!" I shouted above the storm.

I needed everyone to be safe. I had one job—taking care of everyone around me—and I had to get them to our shelter ASAP. Wylie and Benny ran past me, heading toward the shelter behind the main house. I spotted Pris waving at us, Winnie and Boone going down the steps of the shelter and disappearing below.

That left Sky and Dennis.

Sky waved at me as they got out of the van, and I pointed toward Pris, their shouts lost in the wind. My heart pounded as debris kicked up, the sound of a freight train bearing down on us growing louder.

And finally, I spotted Dennis.

"You son of a gun," I yelled, running to him.

Thank god he was a mini horse and I was a strong cowboy. His eyes were wild as I wrapped my arms around him, and he didn't fight me. I knew he was scared.

I needed to get to the storm shelter. I ran as fast as I could, trying not to look at the tornado heading straight for us. Straight toward everything I loved. Everything we had.

It could be gone in a blink.

I went through the gate and rushed toward Priscilla. Sky was the last one to go into the shelter aside from us. Pris was keeping the doors open for me and Dennis.

"Go!" I yelled at her.

I barreled past Pris with Dennis, letting go of our mini disaster. He snorted and trotted straight to Wylie and Boone.

I went back up the steps and helped Pris slam the doors shut. We turned the lock just in time, the door rattling as the wind screeched.

My entire body was shaking, but everyone I loved was accounted for.

Everyone was safe for now.

Pris arms wrapped around me and pulled me back down the steps, everyone hunkering together. I grabbed Sky, dragging them between us as we listened to the storm, everyone silent. Scared.

I sent up a thousand prayers, hoping that everything would be okay. Maybe it would just miss us. Maybe it wouldn't.

Everything shook, the doors rattling violently. I swallowed hard, looking at my siblings. At our friends. My family.

"It's going to be okay," I said calmly. "We're together. We're safe."

Dennis let out a soft, worried neigh.

"I'm sorry," Sky whispered. "I'm so sorry."

"Shh," Pris murmured, holding them close. "It's okay, Sky."

The sound of metal screeching and wood snapping interrupted the horrific sounds of the storm.

But then . . .

It grew more distant.

And then slowly, but surely, it disappeared.

The silence that followed was deafening. Boone breathed out, slumping against Wylie. Billie, Benny, and Winnie melted against the walls of the shelter.

"That was a terrible way to wake up," Billie announced.

That broke the tension. I let out a laugh, and then a groan, a weight lifting off my chest.

We'd made it.

Everyone was safe.

"I'm scared to see the damage," I whispered.

"Whatever it is, we'll handle it," Pris said. "Together."

Everyone agreed.

I stood up and went up the stairs, unlocking the hatch. With a shove, I managed to open it, letting in cool morning air.

Our group emerged from the storm shelter, the sunrise breaking through the dark clouds. Brilliant rays turned the sky peach in the wake of the storm.

I immediately did a three-sixty, feeling relief when I saw the stables and barn. They were fine. From here, the garden looked a little torn up, but we'd work together to help Pris get everything back to order.

The house had lost some roofing. There was some debris strewn around, but otherwise . . .

The ranch looked to be fine.

"I'm gonna go check on the animals," Wylie said.

I nodded. "Let's do a full round-up. Check on it all."

"You got it," Billie said.

Everyone was already breaking apart to do just that. Before I could follow, Pris dragged me close, and then I wrapped my arms around her and Sky, who was shaking.

"That scared me," Pris rasped.

I nodded. "Me too," I croaked.

Tears filled Sky's eyes. "I'm sorry I didn't leave a note. I got a radar alert and wanted to go out and chase it. But I should have left a note. And then when I was out there, one of the tornadoes turned this way."

"We worried for a moment you were gone for good," Pris murmured.

They shook their head, the tears falling as they looked up at both of us. "I knew this morning that this was the place for me. I knew it. And the fear I felt in seeing that tornado come after the people I love . . ."

"*Love*," Pris echoed, swallowing hard.

Sky sniffled. "Yes. *Love*. I love you. Both of you. I know it's fast, I know it's crazy, but I also know it's the truth. I belong here at Rainbow Ranch. I belong here with you."

My mouth dropped in shock. *Love*.

"Does that mean you're here to stay?" Priscilla asked softly.

"I'm here to stay," Sky said. "I'm yours. I'm all yours."

*Love*. They loved us. They were staying.

They were staying at Rainbow Ranch.

"I love you, Sky," Pris said. "I love you, Beau. And you're right, it *is* crazy. It's just as crazy as that damn storm. But it feels right."

"It does," Sky cried.

I was still in shock as the two of them hugged each other and then kissed.

Pris loved me too?

Both of them turned their attention on me.

"Beau," Pris said, raising a brow. "You okay there?"

"Okay?" I breathed out, tears pricking my eyes. "I'm more than okay. I don't have the words. I'm not good with words. But . . ."

I swept the two of them against me, my arms tightening as I held them close. "Welcome home, Sky. I love you. And Pris . . ." I trailed off, looking down at her as the tears fell. "I love you, too. I love both of you so much it hurts."

Pris grinned and leaned up, kissing me hard. "I don't know, Beau. I think you're pretty good with words. What do you think, Sky?"

"I think he is too," they said with a smile.

I kissed them, and then the three of us leaned into each other. Into the love that had taken us by surprise.

"Let's help our family," Pris said. "We got work to do on our ranch."

"Our ranch?" Sky asked.

I nodded and grinned. "*Our* ranch."

# 21
# priscilla

Two Months Later

I LEANED against the fence around the arena, my hat blocking out the summer sun that was shining bright above. Sky was balanced on the top rung and cheering as we watched Beau rush out into the arena on Dolly, his rope swinging through the air as they galloped by the target.

He looped it with ease, earning cheers from the crowd. Billie waited off to the side, wearing a competitive grin. As always, those two were fighting tooth and nail to outperform each other inthe rope tricks portion of the rodeo.

"Go Beau!" Sky shouted.

We both grinned ear to ear as he turned Dolly around, riding her around the edge of the arena and slowing as he came near. The two of us squealed as he swung his rope and aimed at us, the rope looping smoothly around us and pulling us together. Whistles and claps rose from the crowd as he leaned down, planting a kiss on Sky's lips and giving me a flirty masked wink before riding off.

More cheers followed as Billie took to the ring, her wild hair flying as she swung her rope, galloping by on Jasper. Dust kicked up from his hooves. She hit her target with practiced ease and the crowd went wild, stomping their boots on the stadium.

I laughed as Beau went another round. The two kept taking turns until Billie's rope missed—and Beau won.

"Damn," Sky called. "That was a close one."

"It was," I agreed. "I'm sure at some point she'll beat him consistently."

Our masked cowboy ran around the arena a few times and then headed for the gate. Benny opened it, allowing him and Billie out. Now it was time for Wylie's part of the show.

I wrapped my arms around Sky and lifted them, enjoying their squeak as I put their boots to the ground. They tipped their head back with a smile, their lips brushing mine as I stole a kiss.

"Let's go get our cowboy," I said.

They nodded, our fingers intertwining as we walked around the arena toward Beau. He slid off Dolly, giving the gorgeous Palomino Appaloosa an apple as we walked up. Billie was still seated on Jasper, and Benny was standing to the side, adjusting the chaps he wore.

Billie let out a dramatic sigh and shot her older brother a dirty look. "One day, you're gonna stop beating me."

Beau laughed. "Keep dreaming, little sister."

Billie rolled her eyes, but then smiled at the two of us. "Lookee there, now the three of you can be lasso lovebirds."

Our partner laughed, holding out his arms as we both went to him. I leaned my head against his shoulder as I looked over at Billie. "Just you wait. You and Benny are up next."

Billie shook her head. "Not a chance in hell."

"It'll happen when you least expect it," Sky said dreamily.

"Yeah right," Benny snorted. "I think I'm destined to be alone."

"Don't be silly," Beau said. "You'll find someone. Just look at me. Look at Boone."

Our group looked up to see our favorite cook perched on the fence, cheering his partner on as he did laps around the arena.

"Just you wait," Sky said. "Someone will show up at Rainbow Ranch. Someone in need of a place to be loved and feel seen. I don't know if a tornado will bring them to you, but *something* will."

Benny and Billie wrinkled their noses as the crowd erupted again. Beau planted a kiss on the top of my head.

I'd never felt more content.

It'd taken a lot of trust to believe that I'd fall in love again. Sky and Beau had been beyond patient with me, and we'd all learned exactly how good the three of us were for each other.

I finally found the love that saw me and accepted me for who I was.

Our love was the rainbow after the storms that chased us all.

# continue rainbow ranch...

Ready for more Rainbow Ranch? Follow Benny's story in *Saddle Studs* by Max Walker....

# also by clio evans

## Contemporary/Small Town Romance:

CITRUS COVE SERIES

Broken Beginnings (Citrus Cove 1)

Stolen Chances (Citrus Cove 2)

Hidden Roots (Citrus Cove 3)

STANDALONES

Mine: A Reverse Age Gap Romance

The Perfect Gift (Christmas Cuckold Novella)

The Perfect Escape (Summer Spanking Novella)

Lasso Lovebirds: Rainbow Ranch Novella

## Monster Romance:

CREATURE CAFE SERIES

Little Slice of Hell

Little Sip of Sin

Little Lick of Lust

Little Shock of Hate

Little Piece of Sass

Little Song of Pain

Little Taste of Need

Little Risk of Fall

Little Wings of Fate

Little Souls of Fire

Little Kiss of Snow: A Creature Cafe Christmas Anthology

Little Drop of Blood

Little Heart of Stone

Little Spark of Flame

WARTS & CLAWS INC. SERIES

Not So Kind Regards

Not So Best Wishes

Not So Thanks in Advance

Not So Yours Truly

Not So Much Appreciated

FREAKS OF NATURE DUET

Doves & Demons

Demons & Doves

THREE FATES MAFIA SERIES

Thieves & Monsters

Killers & Monsters

Queens & Monsters

Kings & Monsters

GALACTIC GEMS SERIES

Cosmic Kiss

Cosmic Crush

Cosmic Heat

STANDALONES

Nocturnal

# about clio evans

A lover of myths, legends, BDSM, and queer joy in media—
Clio Evans is the author of the Citrus Cove Series, Creature
Cafe Series, Warts & Claws Series, and more.

From Austin but now living in Chicago, they can
always be found drinking coffee or thinking about the
perfect kinky happy ending for their books.

Join them on Instagram, Facebook, TikTok, or their
newsletter for new releases, updates, and more!

www.clioevansauthor.com